BLACK GAMBIT

'A gripping story, well-written . . .
Excellent first thriller by a former diplomatic
correspondent.'

Harpers Queen

'Makes the pulse race.'

Publishers Weekly

'I would put it in the top class of its kind.'

The Oxford Times

'A readable and exciting book that indicates
Eric Clark's name will crop up again in the
future.'

Newsagent & Bookshop

**Also by the same author,
and available in Coronet Books**

THE SLEEPER

Black Gambit

Eric Clark

CORONET BOOKS
Hodder and Stoughton

First published in Great Britain 1978 by
Hodder and Stoughton Limited

Coronet edition 1979
Second impression 1980

Printed and bound in Great Britain for
Hodder and Stoughton Paperbacks, a
division of Hodder and Stoughton Ltd,
Mill Road, Dunton Green, Sevenoaks,
Kent (Editorial Office: 47 Bedford
Square, London, WC1 3DP) by
Richard Clay (The Chaucer Press) Ltd,
Bungay, Suffolk

ISBN 0 340 24271 X

For Rachael and her grandparents

GAMBIT: A chess move in which a player voluntarily sacrifices one or more pawns in an attempt to gain long term advantage.

ACKNOWLEDGEMENTS

Many people in several countries helped me in researching the background to this book. A number of them, mostly present of past employees of government agencies, expressly asked to remain faceless.

I thank them, as I do those I can name:

In the United States, William and Lori Jordan, investigators, and Roger L. Simon; in Holland, Sue and Anton Koene, KLM Royal Dutch Airlines, the staff of Schipol Airport and in particular M. N. Wartena; in Britain, Iain Elliott, editor of *Soviet Analyst*, Dr A. G. Marshall, pathologist, Dr Dennis Evans, of the Imperial College of Science and Technology, William Millinship, former Washington correspondent of *The Observer*, and the Chess Centre.

Finally, there are four people whose encouragement throughout meant so much: my friend and fellow author Raymond Hawkey, Helena, Maureen McConville, and—above all—my wife Marcelle who had faith.

CHAPTER 1

Viktor Michaelovich Pavlinov, junior lieutenant KGB, tried to huddle further back in the archway and wondered yet again whether he dared flick his lighter to check the time.

He decided not. He was proud of the lighter—an American Zippo, a present from his brother-in-law who travelled abroad a great deal—and using it gave him real pleasure. But first he would have to fumble with the layers of clothes, and then it was possible that those in the car would see the light and make an unfavourable mental note.

In any event it could only be minutes now before he was relieved and allowed back into the tobacco-heavy warmth of the car.

In the snow and the darkness he could not see the car, though it was only a street's width away. Lights were never wasted in Moscow's side streets, particularly in an area like this, the old part of town. Once he saw a cigarette-end make an arc and knew it must have been thrown from a window.

Even in the twenty or so minutes he had been outside the car, the cold had worked into his body. He was dressed against it, but at this time of year and at this time in the morning, perhaps an hour from dawn, nothing could provide real protection.

This was his first major assignment since he joined the Fifth Directorate, but so far it had involved nothing more than straightforward surveillance. In four hours, he and the others had taken turns leaving the unmarked Volga and standing in the archway of the cobbled courtyard.

Surely something must happen soon. He could just make out the outline of the building containing the flats on the far side of the courtyard. It was a pre-Revolutionary mansion that would once have housed a single rich family and their servants.

Pavlinov's job was to watch the entrance to the block, an exercise that struck him as pointless for two reasons. For one thing, he could not see that far; for another he was sure that the *upravdom* was sitting inside even now, his door ajar ready to signal if anyone passed.

In all blocks, the *upravdom*—the apartment manager, concierge, and rent collector—was expected to watch the activities of his tenants. Usually his reports were to the local militia. In this case, since the block housed the Zorins, he dealt with the KGB.

To turn his mind from the cold, Pavlinov began to think of Zorin. Every member of the Fifth Directorate was well-briefed on those men the Western press insisted on calling 'dissidents'. The Directorate had, in fact, been set up five years ago to deal with this very problem. More recently it had established within itself a department to deal specifically with Jews who wanted to emigrate.

For many reasons Alexandrai Zorin was regarded as special. He had become a dissident comparatively late; he was not one of those who had become embroiled in the new human rights movement at its birth, eight years before, when the writers Daniel and Sinyavsky were sentenced to concentration camps for writing without a permit and publishing their work abroad.

Zorin had been drawn in trying to protect friends who had become involved. Then he married Tanya, a Jewess. Now he was an important linking figure between the fragmented groups within the dissident movement: scientists, writers, intellectuals, Ukrainians, Crimean Tartars and, of course, the Jews. His name might not be as widely known abroad as that of other dissidents, but among them —and to the authorities—Zorin's importance was immense. If there was a protest, he was likely to be one of the organisers; if there was a new campaign to create publicity in the Western press, he was almost certainly an instigator; if there was an illegal meeting, he was probably the co-ordinator. Through it all he stayed in the background. Even the Western newspapermen whom he manipulated so well knew of him vaguely, if at all.

Pavlinov recalled items from the file. Zorin was forty-one, former Party member (and organiser), married, no children, geneticist, son of the respected Colonel Vladimir Dmitriov Zorin, recipient of the Order of Lenin.

His wife was a fine concert pianist who, until her career had been stopped, seemed likely to win international acclaim. And she was, of course, Jewish. There was even a rumour, noted on her files, that her family had been close to Mrs Meir, in pre-Revolutionary days. Pavlinov hated the Jews. Not, he would stress if he were ever asked, because they were born Jews but because they insisted on remaining a separate group.

And Zorin? He was a scientist, a famous one. It was that among other things that made it impossible for Pavlinov to understand him. Zorin—and his wife—were members of an élite. To dissent, to apply to emigrate ...

Pavlinov knew why. They were greedy. They had much but they wanted more. They wanted the praise of the Western press; they wanted to live well and to slander the Motherland. The pity was that they were allowed to get away with it—for now at least the Party had to appease the West. Furthermore Pavlinov has no doubt that Zorin's late father still had friends where it counted. None of which made the reality any less sickening. Perhaps now that the traitor Solzhenitsyn had been dealt with ...

Pavlinov had just become convinced that he was not to

3

be relieved after the agreed thirty minutes when he saw the other car come into sight. Minutes later he spotted the man who must be his replacement. It was Lissov.

The voice was a whisper, an unnecessary precaution.

'This is it, we're going in. The major says to wait. It won't be long.'

Lissov disappeared in the snow, no doubt back to the warmth of the car.

Pavlinov could do nothing but stand and stamp his feet, and hurt with cold. At last he began to fumble through his clothes until he found his lighter. No longer able to resist, he lit it. It was 7.11, still nearly a half hour from dawn.

Alexandrai Leonidovich Zorin woke five minutes before the alarm was set to go off. He lifted himself on one elbow, leaned over and pressed the button to prevent it ringing.

At 7.25 the first glimmers of light showed through the red curtains covering the one small window. Most other people in the block would be up already, many of them checking their watches as they finished breakfast or wondering whether there was time for more tea. But Zorin's time was more or less his own. He could indulge his preference for starting later and then working through until the early hours of the next day. It was, he had re-flected more than once, the one gift the authorities had given him the day they took away his right to work.

Zorin eased himself up gently so that his head was supported by his hands clasped behind his neck. He wanted to savour the minutes to full daylight, when he would rise.

He turned his head and looked down at Tanya, still asleep, curled foetus-like on her side. For a while he watched her in the half light, resisting an urge to reach out and stroke the black hair that flowed on the pillow. He did not want to wake her. She had been sleeping badly—worried, he knew, about what they all feared was coming.

Solzhenitsyn had gone. Who next?

The thought ended his feeling of contentment. He rolled gently out of bed, walked to the window, and lifted the edge of the curtain. It was still snowing but easing. Looking down, he was surprised that someone was not already beginning to clear the courtyard. There was one thing about the Russian state that had to be admired: it knew how to clear snow. Perhaps, he thought as he turned away, the snow was being left on purpose. Another harassment of the homeless alcoholics who gathered there with their bottles of vodka in even the worst of weathers.

He walked through into the only other room, not bothering to pull on a robe over his pyjamas. At the door he turned. Tanya had moved but was still asleep. He closed the door carefully behind him.

They met six years before, at a reception for a visiting Westerner. In those days both of them had been highly acceptable to the authorities. Almost immediately afterwards she went abroad on a concert tour. Zorin was then already thirty-six and had never before formed a strong attachment with anyone. This time, to his surprise, he found himself missing this woman he barely knew. They married less than a year later. Now he simply could not imagine existing without her.

After washing, he looked down at his stomach and then at his face in the wall mirror. He smiled at his reflection: an unlikely looking hero. A Western journal covering the dissident movement had actually called him that. Tanya teased him about it—partly, he knew, to disguise the fear she felt whenever she saw him named in such a context.

Making tea, he found himself thinking about that article. The authorities seemed convinced that it was Tanya who had drawn him into the dissident movement. Of course, it suited them to believe this—after all, how could a man with his background, with such a father, have acted as he did without outside persuasion? Yet he was convinced that the opinion was held genuinely. The article implied the same point. Strange, because he had never been able to understand how anyone could have acquired such a belief. It was not true. He had tried to correct it, not for the sake of truth but because of a vague feeling that it made Tanya more vulnerable: the state must always have its scapegoat.

Zorin made tea and carried his glass to the larger of two armchairs, moved a magazine and sat. Directly in his vision was a pile of books stacked on the floor. He would have to find somewhere to put them. It seemed almost impossible that this room could hold so much: bookshelves, table and chairs, the two armchairs and a sofa that doubled as a bed when friends stayed, two chess sets, books and magazines and pictures ...

It was not that the apartment was small by Russian standards; it was, in fact, large. He knew families of as many as seven people sharing less space. As privileged members of the élite, he and Tanya had once occupied as much space apiece. But they were fortunate to have these rooms, previously occupied by Tanya's aunt. Zorin and Tanya moved in when she died and—so far at least—no one had tried to evict them.

Tanya's piano was squeezed against one wall, at right angles to his desk. It was old and battered, the possession of a child about to learn, not a professional concert pianist. Tanya treasured it none the less. Until she was banned from the rehearsal rooms she had had no piano at home. This one had been bought from a friend, genuinely a child's outgrown object. Zorin sometimes winced at its tone. Yet even this piano was now threatened: encouraged no doubt by the KGB, neighbours had complained. There had been threats that either the piano or the Zorins must go.

Zorin took another sip from the glass of tea and lit a cigarette. He sucked the rich smoke in deeply, enjoying the light-headed giddiness the day's first cigarette always made him feel. There were sounds from the next room: Tanya waking. Then there was silence again. Often she woke, looked around and then fell again into a short, restless sleep...

No, it was not Tanya who had brought him into the movement, although the two had almost coincided in his life. It had all happened in 1969. As with so many Russians, Pasternak's expulsion from the Writers' Union for 'actions incompatible with the calling of a Soviet writer' and even the Sinyavsky–Daniel case left Zorin not so much unmoved as uninterested. What was special about 1969 was not that he felt strongly about *what* was happening, but that for the first time it touched people he knew personally.

The year had been full of so many actions and retaliations that it was hard to recall them all now: attempts by the authorities to get intellectuals to put their names to a public statement in support of the invasion of Czechoslovakia, mass arrests and secret trials, the hounding of his fellow geneticist Zhores Medvedev who led the attack against Stalin's crackpot scientist Lysenko.

Zorin's involvement had been gradual: trying to help one friend, then another; protesting to one official and then insisting on seeing another. It was at this stage that he married Tanya. She was already active in the Jewish dissident movement—at first, she would confess, as an angry reaction at being forced to cut short her foreign tour because Jews suddenly became universally suspect again.

Zorin himself had been able to survive as a dissident without much trouble—a tribute, he suspected, to the power of his father's old friends who protected him, convinced that he was experiencing a temporary aberration inspired by his new wife.

And so they acted not against him but against Tanya. She was suspended from all her duties as a pianist. When

7

she and her friends protested, using Western correspondents to publicise her case, she was expelled from the Musicians' Union. As the months went by, Zorin's involvement in protest became greater. Finally the state acted against him too, but in stages, as though hesitantly. First he was removed—as a 'security risk'—from his post in the biological section of the Atomic Energy Institute. He was offered another job. He took it. Then that ended. There were others, increasingly minor. He applied to emigrate to Israel and even as those jobs disappeared, his application was refused.

He liked to think he had taken the step of applying to emigrate not for himself but for Tanya. He saw how not being able to play affected her; he'd studied her face when she listened to recordings of other musicians—or, worst of all, recordings of her own recitals. He realised the difference beween her situation and that of most other 'confined' dissidents—writers, after all, could still write and even send their manuscripts abroad. What could a performing musician do but wait knowing that each day that went by she was getting less capable?

The snow had stopped. The major led the way from the second car. Altogether they were seven, Pavlinov at the rear.

The door of the block was open. There was no lift. They began to climb the stairs. The steps were stone and their feet clattered in the silence. Although most of the tenants must have been up, no one looked out to satisfy his curiosity at the strange noises.

The Zorins' flat was on the top floor. As they passed the third, a door opened and was quickly closed.

At the top of the last flight, the major stopped and whispered instructions to Pavlinov's superior. He and one other—the ox-like Dubin who belonged to the Seventh Directorate, the people who normally handled the routine

8

job of surveillance—went forward, along the corridor, and stopped outside the door.

Pavlinov had been in pre-dawn raids before, though none involving anyone of the standing of the Zorins. Still, he knew the routine. First there would be the knocks, then the sleepy replies from within, then the threats, finally the entrance and search.

This was different. In the light from one low-powered naked bulb, Pavlinov saw the major nod and Dubin stand back from the door, half turn and lash out with his leg like a mule. The door crashed open on the third kick.

Pavlinov found himself following the others as they ran down the corridor. There was a narrow hallway packed with a jumble of clothes so that no space in the apartment should be wasted, and then a living room. Zorin—Pavlinov recognised him from his photograph—was standing beside a small desk, facing the door, a pencil in his hand. A moment later a woman called from the bedroom.

Zorin was shorter than Pavlinov had imagined. He looked tired. His waist was beginning to thicken—middle-age, lack of exercise. His short beard was flecked with silver. But when Zorin stiffened Pavlinov felt the man's strength. The mouth was firm, stubborn almost. But most of all Pavlinov noticed the eyes—pale, pale blue and burning with intensity.

A woman entered the room. Her entrance was a cue for a frozen photograph to become a moving film.

'What is it? What is it?'

Pavlinov turned to watch her. She had pulled on a black robe, sleeves too long, hem trailing the ground. Its size accentuated the tininess of her body, the fragility of her features. Except for her voice, deep even in this emotional moment, she could have been a child.

At a command from the major, the men and—Pavlinov noticed for the first time—one woman took up positions in the flat.

9

'This,' said Zorin, 'is an outrage.' He had been half expecting such a visit. Solzhenitsyn's arrest and expulsion eleven days before was but the most spectacular of this latest wave of attacks against the dissidents; Zorin had heard of raids on perhaps twenty homes in the last week.

He walked across to the telephone. 'Violating my home is a flagrant breach of the Constitution. You are acting illegally.'

He picked up the telephone, started to dial, realised there was no tone.

The major stepped forward and took the receiver from his hand.

'I must ask you to behave reasonably.' He took a paper from his pocket, 'As you see, we have a warrant.'

'You had no need to break the door,' said Zorin.

The reply was so swift that it could have been memorised and rehearsed: 'We forced the door because we had reason to believe you might harm yourself if you were forewarned of our presence.'

The major began to take off his coat. He gestured to the men to begin their search.

'May I see the warrant?' asked Zorin. Tanya had moved beside him.

'But of course.'

'All it says is that it is in connection with Case 68. What is that?'

The major took back the paper. 'You have seen the warrant. You will now please sit down and be quiet while we search.'

They began with the pictures. Zorin had learned from experience that, after initial protest, it was best to try to be calm.

What did they expect to find when they removed the paintings from the walls? Secret messages? Hidden safes?

Books were removed from shelves; there were nods from the major when works printed in the West were

brought to him. These together with foreign mazagines—
Paris Match, Nature even an old copy of the *New Yorker*
—were piled on the floor to be bundled and taken away.

The major began to go through Zorin's desk papers. He
found two passports and flicked through them : dates of
marriage, jobs held with their dates, details of travel ...
Under entry number 3, Zorin's ethnic origin was given as
'Russian'; his wife's entry said simply 'Yevrey'.

Jew.

The major forced himself not to voice aloud the thought
that, on the evidence of the passport entries alone, Zorin
was guilty of at least the crime of parasitism. By law anyone who did not work voluntarily for more than thirty
days was subject to internment in a labour camp or to
exile.

In the bedroom the mattress was removed and prodded.
On a shelf one of the searchers found a small Japanese
tape-recorder. He pressed a button, listened for a moment,
carried it to the major.

The voice was unmistakable. The writer Gallich.
Similar tapes had been found in the homes of many intellectuals. When there were not tapes there were often
transcripts of the words. Once Gallich had been a successful playwright; now he wrote and sang these simple songs
lampooning Soviet life.

> My hand had grown thin from shaking hands good-
> bye
> Leave, but I'll remain,
> In this land I'll remain.
> Someone must disdain weariness
> And stand watch over the peace of our dead.

The major switched off the machine.

The search lasted just over three hours. In the end
there were seven piles of belongings stacked near the door
—records, books, notes, photographs, magazines.

Zorin was frightened. The KGB had never before removed so many of his possessions. There had been the odd notebook, an imported novel—even, once, a street map of Moscow, printed in Hungary and given to Zorin by a visiting friend because maps were so hard to obtain in Russia. Zorin, wondering whether the items now gathered together would ever be returned, said nothing.

His possessions were thrown into sacks. The sacks removed.

Zorin and his wife sat waiting for the KGB men to go. His arm was around her shoulders and he felt her trembling, not, he knew, with fear but with rage. He smiled down at her, at the delicate face with the high cheekbones and the skin that looked as though it had never seen sun. He never ceased to marvel at the contradiction between the way she looked and moved and her immense inner strength. Many times he had drawn from that strength, felt himself recharged by her calmness and optimism.

It seemed the search was almost over. The KGB men, thought Zorin, were waiting only for the return of the major. He had left the flat, no doubt to call his superiors.

When the major came back he was abrupt. 'You will come with me.'

Zorin squeezed Tanya, released her and stood.

To her he said, 'You know who to call.'

He nodded to the major to signify he was ready.

'No,' said the major. 'You don't understand. You will *both* come with me.'

Zorin felt the anger rising. 'Why her? What has she done?'

He felt Tanya reach for and squeeze his hand.

'It'll be all right,' she whispered.

The major's voice softened. 'Your wife is right. Please, do not refuse. I would only have to insist. I do not want to have you dragged to the car.'

Outside, the streets were being cleared of snow. The

Zorins were placed in separate cars. 'Where are you taking us?' asked Zorin. No one answered. The other car moved off. 'Where is my wife going?'

'Lefortovia,' answered the driver.

'Quiet!' snapped the major. 'No one will speak to the prisoner.'

The word made Zorin shudder. 'So I am a prisoner?' It was a silly remark, he knew, but it was easier to speak than remain silent.

CHAPTER 2

Robert Sunnenden squared the files on the right-hand corner of his desk and admired again his new office.

When Henry Kissinger had become Secretary of State, Robert Sunnenden had moved with him from the White House to the State Department. He preferred his new quarters at State. They were larger and more luxurious and he was a man who believed in the signs of status. More important, he felt removed from the stigma of Watergate.

As a member of Kissinger's staff Sunnenden had no direct contact with the scandal. But as the months went by, Watergate affected everyone in the building. It was, he had explained to Janet, like being a non-smoker in a room where others were smoking cigars. To outsiders, your clothes reeked of tobacco smoke too.

On the morning of 24 February Sunnenden had more than his office to please him. It really began to look as though he was a coming man. Two days before he learned that he was expected to join Kissinger on his new mission to the Middle East. And he was working today, a Sunday, only because the Secretary had singled him out.

Kissinger was lunching later in the day with the Egyptian Foreign Minister. Sunnenden had been asked to briefly set down the likely major developments in the Middle East now, some five months after the Yom Kippur War. The request came at the last minute, almost as an afterthought. But he had been asked, and that was what mattered.

Sunnenden had just finished. His memorandum was

short but he had been working on it virtually non-stop since the telephone call last night. The Secretary might only glance at it, or ignore it completely—but if he read it, the report had to be good.

Now the note was on its way to Kissinger's home. Sunnenden sat at his desk, re-reading a carbon copy. He nodded. Yes, it was good. Short, but not too short. Dogmatic? Certainly, but justified by his knowledge of US–Soviet affairs. His note concentrated on the Middle East in that context—his own speciality and, fortunately, Dr Kissinger's major interest.

It was not yet 10.30. Sunnenden was reluctant to go home despite his exhaustion. The boys would be out swimming. Friends were coming to brunch at one. There was nothing to do until then. He could lie on a sofa and read *The Post*. But the building held him. The near emptiness, the quiet, made it and the few people there special.

Besides, he had to admit to himself that there was some relief in being away from Janet for a few hours, much as he treasured her and their marriage. Her belief in him, her ambition for his future, had always been one of the characteristics about her that most pleased him; no one had shown them before. But since the occasion six months before when he had bungled a key assignment for the Secretary—through overconfidence he had prepared a brief that neglected to take two major points into account —it had become one that harassed him. He felt driven, not urged: under constant test. When she had learned of the Middle East trip, and then this latest task, her reaction had been not of contentment but of concern that he should not make another mistake.

Sunnenden forced his mind back to the office, slightly guilty at his thoughts. He owed Janet a lot. He carefully squared the carbon copy, knowing that he would take it home for her to read.

His desk was nearly empty, as always. It was one of the traits that had led colleagues at Defense to call him, not lovingly, the Computer. The other was his gift for producing, assembling and analysing facts at very short notice.

He knew what they called him—and why—but he was proud of the nickname. His methods made sense. You completed one task and then started another. If, occasionally, you had to lay aside a task for a more urgent one, you left the papers in full view as a constant reminder to get the job done as soon as possible.

There was one such reminder in front of him now: a buff folder filled with photostats, newspaper clippings, extracts from embassy reports, and notes. Sunnenden carried it to the window. Outside, Washington was almost deserted.

Being one of the few people working that day gave him a warm feeling of self-importance. Sunnenden was not short—he was a little over medium height—but he behaved like a small man, pushing, fighting to prove his worth. The son of a naval petty officer, he had gone to the wrong colleges, grown up with the wrong people—and battled his parents' fear that he was too ambitious. That was where Janet's convictions of his talents and future, forcibly voiced, had been so important.

Sunnenden walked across to an easy chair and looked around the room. This was the first time in his life he had had an office on which he could impose his own personality—or, rather, the personality he wanted to communicate.

He tried to wear his surroundings like a well-tailored suit. Janet had helped him decorate the room: the piece of Eskimo sculpture on the coffee table, the plaster bust of Karl Marx set next to the rows of books on Communism and Russia, the computer drawings on the wall ...

16

No matter what they said, he *had* made it. He'd done well at Defense, even if he had been disliked. Now, thanks to Allan Scott, he could do even better.

Sunnenden lifted the file. He would, he decided, spend an hour or two working on it. He could then have his notes waiting on Scott's desk the next morning.

Sunnenden took his spectacles from his shirt pocket, perched them near the end of his nose and glanced at the first page of the file.

The dossier concerned Russian dissidents. Most of the data was familiar: Solzhenitsyn's expulsion and his progress through Europe; other arrests, still it seemed, continuing; feature articles on psychiatric hospitals in the USSR ... Separate reports outlined reactions to the Soviet Union's moves against dissidents. Another report, put together by the CIA with the help of a 'friendly' journalist, covered the thinking of the powerful American Jewish interests and their various possible reactions.

Sunnenden read quickly, making terse notes on the cover of the folder. Scott had asked him to look at the subject, and it was Scott, after all, who had brought Sunnenden into the Kissinger team. It was Scott too who had nursed him back into the Secretary's favour after his mistake. By helping Sunnenden to get good assignments, by feeding him useful pieces of information and advice, and by making judicious remarks to others whose views the Secretary also regarded highly, Scott had led the younger man to his present potentially important spot. This time Sunnenden was determined not to fail.

Sunnenden also had to admit it was rewarding to work for Scott. You got feedback, he told you what he thought. Kissinger rarely reacted to anything you did unless it was so bad that he cursed you out publicly.

Scott was in the Secretary's close inner circle, one of the few with direct access to him and, rarer still, one who did not hesitate to tell him the full, unsugared truth. It was Sunnenden's luck that Scott had been present at a Senate Committee hearing at which he had given evidence on the United States' missile capabilities vis-à-vis those of the Soviets'. Scott had been impressed, and as a result Sunnenden had moved from Defense to State.

Scott's job was not defined anywhere. In the internal telephone directory he was described as 'special assistant to the Secretary of State'. He was, in fact, Kissinger's contact with the world, with Congress, with the lobbyists —even with his own staff. The Secretary knew how to save the United States and the world; Scott made sure that no one stepped in the way.

That was why Sunnenden was now poring through the file on dissidents. Scott was concerned about the different American-Jewish pressure groups, to his mind both powerful and effective. Scott wanted Sunnenden's views on what the Soviets were likely to do next. Did the sudden clampdowns, beginning with Solzhenitsyn and followed by a mass of less publicised arrests, reflect a real change in Soviet attitudes?

Re-reading the clippings Sunnenden decided that in the Soviet position he would probably have taken the same action they had against Solzhenitsyn. They could not let him continue; imprisoning him again would have placed the Soviets in a near-impossible diplomatic position.

He was not so sure, though, that he would have followed the writer's expulsion with further arrests. He could see their reasoning: a series of sharp blows to warn the dissidents that the gloves were off. And he deduced that the Soviets expected the Western press to be so full of Solzhenitsyn that the other twenty or thirty arrests and expulsions would attract little attention.

To a large degree they had been right. Public attention had concentrated on Solzhenitsyn. But—and it was here that they had miscalculated—influential groups and individuals in the West had noted each new event. One great flaw in the Soviet decision-making process, he thought—not for the first time—was the inability to understand the strength of pressure groups on Western politicians who had to get re-elected.

To many people it had been the proof they sought that the Soviets really were bastards. To others—it was confirmation of a conviction that the Soviets, not content with destroying the Jews in the Middle East through their Arab puppets, wanted to annihilate them in Russia.

Many American-Jewish interest groups were particularly sensitive just now—cognisant of the fact that Israel itself was going through its greatest crisis since independence, and also deeply suspicious of Kissinger. To some of them he was a reluctant Jew leaning over backwards to act pro-Arab.

Scott's concerns were twofold: to protect the policies that the Secretary—and he—believed in, and to anticipate and negate any attacks that might be brewing. Watergate made it all harder. Dr Kissinger himself was riding high at the moment, but the press and the people were now ready to tear down their leaders.

Sunnenden returned to his desk and dictated a one-page memorandum. The Soviet actions, he said, would undoubtedly create extra tensions and resultant pressures at home among some legislators. To counter this, some token gesture might be politically useful. Perhaps, for example, the question of the rights of dissidents could again be raised with the Soviet Ambassador. Such a step, he thought, would not have any practical effect. But if the attempt could be given full publicity, perhaps that alone would be helpful at home.

Sunnenden, dictating in clipped tones, went on without pause to the second half of his memorandum: his assessment of the Soviets' future policy on the subject and its implications for the United States. He was brief and dogmatic. The hard-line attitude at home was meant to satisfy the Soviet hawks, but it should mean that their leaders could practise a softer line abroad. On the dissident question much, of course, depended on how long the arrests continued, how widespread they were, and just *who* they included. But he would expect it to be comparatively short lived, to be followed by a quiet period and then, ultimately, by even more repressive policies.

Sunnenden played back the tape, decided he was satisfied, and locked the cassette in the wall safe for transcription the next morning.

By the time he had checked out past the guard, he had dismissed the subject. He was thinking about travelling with the Secretary to the Middle East.

The major remained silent as the car headed north through the Moscow streets past the Academy of Arts, the Tolstoy Museum and the Soviet Peace Committee. There was a strong smell of human bodies in the car.

Traffic was surprisingly heavy and despite the five lanes the car had to slow at the busy corner with Kalinin Prospekt. As they neared Gorky Street, the major muttered something to the driver. The next moment Zorin heard the siren. Other cars pulled to the side and the Chaika swept through on the outside lane.

Zorin's main anxiety was for Tanya. On previous occasions they had left her alone. His worry for her was almost a sickness in his stomach. If they hurt her . . .

The heater had cleared the side windows of ice. Zorin could now see the massive granite statue of Karl Marx opposite the Bolshoi and their destination became obvious. It was confirmed when the car began to slow in Dzerzhinsky Square. Above it towered another statue, of Dzerzhinsky himself, the first post-Revolutionary head of secret police.

They reached a courtyard in the old section. A militiaman examined papers and then the car was through. On one side of the courtyard was Zorin's destination, Luby-anka Prison.

For the first time he began to feel real fear, for himself as well as Tanya.

Zorin was handed over at the entrance, like a parcel. Two warders, obviously expecting him, signed a paper which the major folded and placed in his breast pocket. For a moment it looked as though he would speak; then he turned and walked back to the car.

Zorin was led through two sets of gates, and into a bare room. He was ordered to strip and to put on a striped pyjama-type uniform, taken to what was obviously the prison hospital and given an examination. He might, but for the circumstances, have been going through an annual medical check-up at work.

There were two doctors. After each test—for blood pressure, reflexes, teeth—they made notes. Zorin tried asking questions. Only one answered. All he said was 'Yes, fine, fine, fine, yes.' The reply was the same whatever the question—'What is this about?' 'Where is my wife?' 'What authority do you have for this?'

Once Zorin walked to the door. They made no effort to stop him. Outside there were guards.

When the tests were completed, one of the doctors pushed a button on a desk. Almost immediately Zorin was led downstairs, below ground. There was a smell of damp and rotting plaster; apart from the footsteps of himself and his escort there was no sound. Finally Zorin was pushed into a box-like cell.

Three of the walls were bare concrete. The fourth consisted of two sets of bars, spaced about six inches apart, rather like those on the cage of a particularly dangerous animal in a zoo. The only light came from a faint bulb above, protected by a wire cage. There was nothing to sit on but the floor. In the thin, baggy prison uniform Zorin felt both cold and exposed.

For a while he crouched on the concrete floor. When it became too uncomfortable he walked to the bars and shouted. There was no reply.

He kept thinking of Tanya. Where was she? What were they doing to her? She had not been well lately, perhaps the result of semi-confinement. He was not religious, but he began to mutter prayers for her safety.

Zorin walked up and down shivering from the combination of cold and hunger. Finally, he curled in a corner. He had been told once—he could not remember where or by whom—that taking and holding a deep breath warmed the body. He tried it a few times. It was a distraction, but all he felt was a slight giddiness.

Time passed. He dozed and walked and recited poems aloud and remembered previous confrontations with the KGB which he had endured. Gradually a kind of numbness took over. Pangs of hunger came and went. He was almost annoyed when he heard voices and then the guards arrived and he was marched away from his cell.

Apart from the fact that there were no windows, the room could have been an office anywhere. Admittedly, the furniture was spartan, but then so it was in many offices.

The walls were plain. There was a green filing cabinet and a row of open shelves on which stood boxes, not books.

The steel desk stood in the centre, facing the door. The top was clear except for a pad and an ashtray. Behind it sat a man in a swivel chair. The chair, bucket shaped and made of imitation leather, was almost certainly imported.

The occupant of the swivel chair was impeccably dressed in a steel-grey suit, a silver and red striped tie.

The man stared at Zorin for several seconds, then he smiled.

'It would be nice to start by introducing myself,' he said, 'since I know you are Alexandrai Leonidovich. But'

—and he paused to spread his hands in a gesture—'it is perhaps better that you think of me simply as a friend. A nameless friend.'

He was still smiling.

He leaned forward, elbows on the desk. 'It may surprise you but I am an admirer of yours.' He paused to let Zorin absorb his words. 'Yes,' he added, 'I thought you right and brave when you called attention to the effect radiation was having on people in our northern territories. That's what we want—people who are right and brave.'

His tone became conspiratorial. 'Of course we know there were those who did not like it. What man of any fire has no enemies?'

Zorin's chair was cutting into his back; he wanted to lean forward, but the desk was too far away.

The man opened a drawer of the desk, took out a thick folder, and began reading. Occasionally he glanced up, a quizzical look on his face.

Zorin decided to try to establish some sort of initiative. 'Where is my wife? I insist on knowing. Our Constitutional rights have been—'

The interrogator's fist hit the desk. 'Can't you understand that you have no rights? That all that stands beween you and ...' He paused, surely to rephrase what he had been about to say.

He stood and walked around the desk and sat on the edge, looking down at Zorin.

'Can you not see that this time you are in real trouble?' He raised his hand to stop any reply. 'Let me continue. Then I will let you talk. You have done such foolish things.' His voice was full of simulated hurt. 'Oh yes, you are a fool. Even great scientists are human. Can't you accept that—that you can make mistakes just as others can?'

He returned to the desk and opened the file, flicking pages and reading isolated paragraphs aloud.

'Moscow University, a good student and Party member; political organiser . . .

'Brilliant researcher, but signs of delusions of infallibility . . .

'Arrested 28 July 1973. Charge—hooliganism. Sentence—fifteen days, extended by ten days after striking another prisoner.'

The interrogator looked up: 'Provoked, were you? It happens. I told you you have enemies. All the more reason you need friends, eh?'

Zorin tried to work out a background for his interrogator. If he could make him a person, he would be easier to resist. Age, perhaps thirty, thirty-one. Rank, well, he was young but very assured. Lieutenant-Colonel? Or was that too high?

He concentrated on the accent. Certainly not Moscow. That soft 'th' pointed to the south. Perhaps near the Ukraine? The Rostov area?

The interrogator swivelled in his chair. "Alexandrai Leonidovich, it is a time for being honest, yes? First, I will be honest. Then you.'

He walked to the door and barked an order for tea which arrived almost immediately. Zorin rose to reach for his but was waved back. 'No, you must sit. There are rules.'

Zorin took the tea, stirred in the spoonful of fruit jelly and sipped. It tasted good. He wondered if he should ask for food. He had already decided he would not take cigarettes even if they were offered. Their withdrawal when it came would give the KGB yet another weapon.

The interrogator began walking up and down.

'To be honest, then.

'One'—he checked the number with his fingers—'you have done many stupid things for which you could and should be punished.'

He waited for a reaction which did not come.

24

'Two, you have enemies.

'Three, the cause you pursue is doomed anyway.

'Four, the penalties you face are severe.'

His voice rose. 'What *are* those stupid things? You have fermented unrest, you have consorted with the Zionists who oppose peace, you have passed information to our enemies . . .'

'I have passed nothing. I . . .'

'*Who* are your enemies? You might think we all are. But no, there are some who think you are a good man who has been foolish.' He clasped his hands in front of his face. 'Believe me, Alexandrai Leonidovich, we want to help you.

'I said you cause—cause, what a grand word!—is doomed. Can you deny it yourself? What is your own toast, eh?'

He waited for Zorin to prompt him on the bitter wording of the toast the dissidents used among themselves. When there was no reaction, he spoke it himself: 'To the success of our hopeless enterprise.

'And the penalties . . .' his voice dropped. 'Well, let us leave that. It is up to you, Alexandrai Leonidovich, to make that unnecessary.'

He took a single sheet of paper from the file and handed it to Zorin.

'Where is my wife?'

'Please, first read the paper.'

It was a confession, an apology and a renunciation. It began with a listing of his confessed crimes against the Soviet people, some real, some false: passing information to Western correspondents, smuggling manuscripts abroad, publishing clandestine literature . . . Zorin tried not to show by his expression which specific charges were true and which were not.

He now realised, read the paper, that he had been wrong, and he asked for forgiveness and understanding.

It mentioned his father and the pain he must have caused him. He had been a loyal citizen, a good Party worker, until he met his wife. She had encouraged him into activities and beliefs that he now knew were wrong. He realised that she had been used as a tool by the Zionist reactionaries she met while visiting abroad as a pianist.

At the bottom was a space for Zorin's signature.

He looked up and for the first time since the session began started to smile.

'You really expect me to sign this?'

The door opened behind him and he heard a second man enter.

His interrogator took back the paper, placed it on the desk facing Zorin, and gathered up his file.

His voice was very slow; his tone resigned. 'I did not want to hand you over to the specialists. I tried.'

He began to walk past Zorin.

'Oh yes, Alexandrai Leonidovich,' he murmured half to himself, 'you will sign. If not now, later. If not today, tomorrow. If not this week, next. But you will sign. Yes, you will sign."

The next interrogator ordered Zorin to stand. When he remained seated he called in two guards who pulled Zorin to his feet. Then the interrogator hit him across the face with the back of his hand, just hard enough to establish his commanding role.

'When I say stand, you will stand.'

Something in Zorin snapped. The moment the guards released his arms he threw himself forward, his hands outstretched grasping for the interrogator's neck.

He did not reach that far. The blow hit him in the middle of the back and sent him forward into the desk. The guards pulled him to the floor and one kicked him viciously in the ribs.

'Good,' he heard the interrogator say, 'now we know

one another. The foolishness of treating you as an honoured guest is over.'

The questioning seemed to continue for hours. The guards remained in the room. Whenever Zorin began to sleep on his feet one or other of them hit him in the back or across the shoulder with a club.

He could see the confession still lying on the desk, but the new interrogator made no attempt to get him to sign it.

Now he was asking how the dissidents communicated to arrange a meeting. What were the arrangements about using the telephone?

'I know nothing of what you are talking about.'

The interrogator came forward, his hand lifted, his voice rising in anger.

Zorin heard the door open again. He was sure it would be the first interrogator again—the timeless ploy of alternating the friendly questioner and the cruel one.

It was a third interrogator, in his way as chilling as the one who now left.

'I want you to know that I do not care if you say anything or nothing,' he announced. 'You are doomed. You will never leave here.'

He sat reading papers, as Zorin continued to stand in front of him, fearing the blows even more than he desperately wanted sleep.

After perhaps an hour the interrogator reached over and touched the confession with his finger tips. 'You will sign now?'

Zorin did not reply.

'Very well.' And again he sat mute.

Altogether there were four interrogators including the 'kind' one. They came and went in different permutations, staying for varying lengths of time.

Sometimes they talked—cool, angry, gently, conspiratorially. Sometimes there was silence.

Zorin knew the cruel/kind technique of interrogation.

27

It was a cliché. But none the less he found himself succumbing to it. Each time the door opened to herald a change of interrogator he found himself hoping it was the first one.

The man was sympathetic. 'Surely you can see why your visa application had to be refused? You are a special man, a great geneticist...'

Coaxing. 'Renounce. That's all. Everything will be forgiven. Just sign.'

Scornful. 'Why waste yourself like this? Within days of signing you can be back doing real work—the kind you like. You owe it to yourself and your talent.'

He could be pragmatic. 'You educated liberals—you are an entirely unrepresentative minority. Oh yes, the West has protected you till now—they like to think real Soviets are like you, that you are the great silent majority suddenly speaking out. Fools. You don't believe that.' Zorin said nothing, but had to admit to himself that the interrogator was right. 'And now,' he added, 'even there you are now an embarrassment. They too want détente. The Americans found Solzhenitsyn as troublesome as we did.'

And occasionally he could appear saddened. 'There are those who think you should be charged with treason.' The maximum penalty for which, of course, was death.

Through it all Zorin thought of Tanya: was she suffering the same threats, the same treatment?

He was terrified that she was. After his early questioning, he ceased asking because he did not want them to realise how great was his fear and concern. Then as the days passed he had to ask. None of the KGB men replied. He realised not knowing was part of his torture. The KGB let his mind paint its own nightmare picture of what it thought might be happening.

On one occasion Zorin had to force himself not to volunteer his co-operation if they would produce Tanya unharmed. He reminded himself it would achieve nothing: if she had been harmed there was no way that it could be undone. If she had not, he would simply be giving his captors an idea. He did know that if they produced Tanya and gave him an ultimatum, sign or she will be tortured, he would give way. Beside her, nothing mattered. —

Time became meaningless. Zorin was taken back to his cell on two occasions and allowed to sleep, but he did not know for how long. There was neither day nor night. There were no sounds other than those of the doors opening or closing to let interrogators in or out.

In the interrogation room the physical violence was never acute: a sharp push, a blow in the back when he started to slump. The pain, though, lay in the standing and in the degradation. His legs had begun to swell and to lose all power of feeling. And he soon learned that the kindness of hot tea was, in time, a cruelty.

He bore the need to urinate until, at last, he was forced to ask to be taken to a lavatory. The fact that his request had been made did not even register on the interrogator's face. He happened to be the silent one, but Zorin found later that none of the interrogators, not even the 'kind' one, would let him out of the room.

Finally he had to urinate where he stood. For a few seconds the warmth of the wet urine was actually a pleasure: the pain had reached a point where he had been sure his bladder would burst. Then came the smell and the cold and the feeling of shame—the small boy who had wet his pants.

One of the interrogators spent one session doing nothing but read out names: Vladimir Bukovsky ... Petr Grigorevich ... Viktor Fainberg ...

The names went on.

Zorin made no comment on them. There was none he could have made. They were all men who had gone—im-

29

prisoned or locked in psychiatric hospitals or sent into exile.

To hear their names brought a sadness; it made him realise just how isolated those who remained were becoming. So many good men had been lost.

Then came the moment when Zorin realised a crucial point had been reached. The 'kind' interrogator entered the room, but the other one did not leave. They whispered together and then one pressed the buzzer for more guards.

The 'kind' one shrugged at Zorin. 'I am sorry,' he said, 'I have done all I could.'

The guards moved forward to grasp Zorin's arms and turned him abruptly towards the door. The interrogator signalled to the guards to wait, walked over to Zorin and stood facing him.

'You won't believe it,' he said, 'but I really have had your welfare at heart.'

The guards led Zorin nearer the door. Again the interrogator made them stop.

'You know the trouble,' he said. 'You intellectuals— you love to suffer. You always have. You always will.'

CHAPTER 3

Allan Scott eased the belt of his trousers another notch and sighed with relief.

Then he put his feet back on the leather topped writing table and continued listening to the tape.

Scott had made a conscious point of following the Kissinger Middle East tour through newspaper reports and Washington cocktail talk instead of the official information that poured back to the White House and the State Department.

He read—and he listened. He noted the universal approval when the Secretary took the Israeli prime minister a list of Israeli prisoners being held in Syria. The following day he listened even more closely when the expected announcements came, reporting that American–Egyptian diplomatic relations were being resumed and that President Nixon was being invited to Cairo.

He avoided diplomatic and intelligence reports and assessments simply because as a political animal, he wanted to view the Secretary's visit the way the voters would, not as some privileged insider.

What he needed, though, was the feel of the situation in Israel. He could have gone himself, but he rarely travelled now. The Secretary tried to persuade him to do so —the last time had been Dr Kissinger's secret visit to Peking which Scott had not been able to resist. He now pleaded that he could not afford to be away from Washington. In reality, he had developed a fear of flying—or, more precisely, of flying over water. Surely he was more useful back in Washington where he could gauge reactions to the latest news and developments and try to encourage or thwart them.

And, of course, this time he had Sunnenden alongside the Secretary.

Throughout his working life, Scott had made a point of looking out for bright young men. Once he helped them, they became *his* men, even when they moved way out of his field of direct influence. He now had a network of such men. A perceptive colleague had once dubbed him 'the Godfather of Washington', although that was not strictly accurate—his tentacles reached out beyond that city. But his strength came not from this alone, but from the fact that he never used his influence for personal gain or prestige.

Sunnenden's overpowering desire for status and recognition amused Scott. It also pleased him, Ambition was one thing all his protégés had in common. He did not have to like them, only to trust their judgment and believe they were going to get somewhere.

Though Scott enjoyed power, he did not want it for its own sake. He genuinely believed in the people, policies or cause for which he worked. The beliefs were often simplistic. He believed in the free world, the United States, the Republican Party, the President—and in Dr Kissinger and America's foreign policy under him.

His convictions were obvious and passionate. Often people yielded simply because they were swept up by his open beliefs in a town where convictions often took second place to survival and ambition.

His appearance helped: he was a fat man who had once been a fat child and before that a fat baby. He was sure that this had determined his behaviour: a fat boy must go out of his way to get on with other kids to survive and overcome their teasing. He had also found it true that people trusted a fat man—Shakespeare was right. Scott suspected that a disproportionate number of con men were probably fat.

Now, two days after Kissinger's return from the Middle East, Scott was sitting in his apartment in Foggy Bottom.

The apartment—with its furnishings—was the phoniest thing about him. When he had moved into it, he had called an interior designer. His instructions had been brief: 'Make it look *American.*' The result was Colonial furniture, paintings depicting great moments in US history and—Scott's touch—photographs of a dozen or more American folk heroes, from Billy Graham to John Wayne, all signed. It was all so theatrical, so overstated, that it worked.

Scott was listening to a tape of his conversation with Sunnenden the previous evening. The voice-activated recorder was built into an ornamental inkstand that stood on the writing desk. Scott taped most of his business conversations at the apartment—which was where much of his real work took place—to listen for nuances or leads that he might have missed during the conversation itself. Quite often, as a result of this practice, he had amended his reading of what the other party really meant.

Scott had taped Sunnenden, however, for a different reason. He had been so tired that he doubted his ability to absorb what Sunnenden had to tell him. Yet Scott felt he needed to talk to him. The disappearance of the two dissidents, the Zorins, and the refusal of the Soviets even to confirm they were being held in prison, had made a bad situation worse. He gathered from Dunn at the White House that the Jewish pressure groups were leaning a little harder on the President. With 1976 not far away, groups that could deliver votes *and* money were not to be disregarded.

Scott knew, though, that what Kissinger was doing was right; in his policies lay the only hope for the Middle East —for the Israelis as well as for the Arabs. 'Now,' he muttered to himself, 'all I have to do is convince them.'

The tape reached the point where, pleasantries over, Sunnenden was answering Scott's questions. By now Scott had read the various reports, had talked however briefly with Kissinger himself. But what he wanted from Sunnenden was the *feel*, the asides, the things you never got in memoranda or in briefings.

Sunnenden was talking about the atmosphere in Israel. 'I'd expected it to be bleak,' he said, 'but nothing prepared me for the way it was.'

He began listing points and even if Scott had not been present when the recording had been made, he would have known from the clipped nature of Sunnenden's voice that he was ticking them off as he spoke.

At first he spoke briefly, confining himself to concise answers to Scott's questions: yes, he agreed, he had been surprised by the amount of anti-Kissinger feeling in Israel. Gradually he became more expansive.

'The strongest feeling that came across,' said the taped voice, 'was the belief that Dr Kissinger wanted détente with Russia at any price—even if it meant Israel's paying it. Most of the people I talked with were convinced we'd actually let the fighting go on until it looked as though the Israelis were getting the upper hand. *Then* we'd moved in —to stop them from getting too strong a position, because we needed a stalemate to make postwar negotiations easier.'

As the tape went on, the voice began to relax: a consequence of time, the lateness of the hour, and of the drink the two men were sharing.

Sunnenden told of advertisements in Israeli newspapers, placed to coincide with Kissinger's visit: 'Senator Jackson: Stop Kissinger,' public praise for the Senator's strong anti-Soviet line, and condemnation of what was seen as Kissinger's soft and anti-Jewish policies.

As he grew more expansive, Sunnenden gave Kissinger's nickname in the Israeli press: the 'mini Metternich'.

And he described a conversation with an Israeli broadcaster who spoke with a smile but obviously meant what he said: 'I wish that man would get married. Then he could start fucking a woman instead of us Jews.'

Sunnenden turned to the Zorins whose name had also recurred in conversations. 'It was as if ...' Sunnenden seemed to be forcing himself to think through something he had not considered before. 'Well, as if people needed to focus on one single understandable thing. You follow?' There was no audible reply; Scott must have confined himself to nodding his head. 'It wasn't that the Zorins mattered. It was the fact that they provided an easily assimilated, a highly emotive, example of what the Russians thought of the Jews—those Russians to whom we, the United States, seemed prepared to give everything provided it wasn't ours to lose.'

Scott walked over and switched off the tape. He did not want to hear any more. It made him feel uneasy.

He was an intuitive operator, and the Zorins' arrest on top of everything else made him feel uneasy. It provided too much ammunition for the Secretary's critics. It was potentially embarassing. Dr Kissinger couldn't act—officially. Maybe, an unofficial approach ...

He picked up the telephone and dialled the direct line to his office in the White House. He was answered immediately. 'Helen?' he said, not introducing himself. He spent two minutes making small talk, asking after her health and her husband even though it was only a day since he had last called.

'I want you to do a small thing for me, Helen. Get hold of whoever knows such things—Protocol, maybe—find when's the next reception at the Soviet Embassy, and call me back. Okay? After that, give a call to Bob Sunnenden and ask if he could drop by. No rush. Maybe tomorrow sometime.'

*

Outside the door, Zorin found himself led along a corridor until he could see a glass door and daylight. A guard produced a sack hood, handed it to Zorin and ordered, not unkindly, 'Put it on.'

Zorin wanted to fight, to struggle—at least to make a gesture, no matter how futile. He was too weak, in body and in mind. Wearily, he placed he hood over his head. One of the guards tightened the pull-cords. He found he could breathe easily and, surprisingly, there was a slight glimmer of light, like the coming of dawn.

Zorin was led down two steps and into a car. It pulled away. His face was itching and he began to lift a hand to scratch it. Immediately both hands were grabbed and he felt the cold of handcuffs forced on to his wrists.

After perhaps half an hour the car stopped and he heard a clanking of metal. The car moved forward and then halted suddenly again. It must have passed through gates and entered a courtyard.

He was pulled out with a jerk. Seven stumbling paces, then five steps, then the clank of footsteps on what must have been a corridor.

The smell seeped through the hood: carbolic acid and food, more like a hospital than a prison. Zorin's guard turned right, taking the geneticist with him. A door opened and he was pushed into a room. He half fell and then two sets of hands lifted him and placed him down, face upwards though still covered, on what felt like a table.

The handcuffs were removed. Just at the moment when he felt a brief, irrational pleasure at free hands, they were grasped again. The hands, then his feet were placed in clamps, and his whole body pulled into an X.

He felt heat on his face, more light inside the hood. He knew why when the material was suddenly lifted away: around him was a battery of blinding lights.

The table he was lying on might have been an operating table. Turning his head to the left he could make out an oxygen mask. There was movement and he realised there were many people in the room.

Zorin closed his eyes and tried to breathe deeply and steadily. Treat it as you did the dentist when you were a child, he told himself. Focus on other things. He started to remember a poem.

The voice, muffled like the shape of the person speaking, cut into the poem.

'You are in the Serbsky Institute,' it intoned, naming the most notorious psychiatric prison hospital in Moscow. 'A preliminary diagnosis shows that you are suffering from paranoia and megalomania. You seem to suffer from an obsessive delusion that you are a champion of truth and justice. As doctors, it is our duty to help you to overcome that delusion.'

Two outstretched arms came within the circle of light. One hand held a small pair of scissors which were used to cut a gap in Zorin's shirt, just below the inside of the elbow. The hand retreated and re-emerged with a swab which was wiped over the skin. It appeared a third time with a hypodermic which the hand held a few inches from his arm.

The voice began again. 'I want to show you that we can help you ... if we find the need. You will not like the drug we are about to give you, but if you consider carefully you will realise that it is for your own good. When you have wrong thoughts, we can give you this drug. When your thoughts are good, well ... there are rewards.'

The voice addressed the figure next to it. 'Go ahead now.'

Zorin began to struggle, pulling his wrists against the clamps as the needle came nearer and slid in.

'The drug is called succinylcholine,' the voice said. 'It ... well, you will see in thirty to forty seconds.'

Zorin knew. Succinylcholine, a derivative of the South American poison curare, was a paralysing drug, used in major surgery—when the patient was under anaesthetic. It had also been used, Zorin knew, on patients undergoing electro shock treatment to stop their breaking limbs when shocks were administered.

Zorin thought he felt the numbness in his toes first but perhaps that was anticipation. Knowing what would happen only made it worse. The drug would paralyse his body, starting with the small, rapidly moving muscles and progressing until, finally, it paralysed the diaphragm and he could no longer breathe. And all the time he would be fully conscious—able to see, hear and feel.

In short, he was going to feel himself die.

There was no doubt now: the drug was starting to work. He felt it in his eyes, then almost immediately in his fingers. He tried to move, tensing himself against the clamps, but could not. He took a deep breath, then another. The third time he tried to breathe he couldn't. He felt his head swelling; there was a tightness, a bursting across his chest. He wanted to scream, to plead, to yell to God. Nothing. He tried to close his eyes; the lids stayed open. There were lights and faces. His temples were pounding now. He could smell blood, high in his nostrils. He was going to split apart like a paper bag. This was what drowning must be like, or death in space, or being buried alive ... 'God, please, please let me die!'

He was swimming into unconsciousness now. A relief. Then a hand came out, and a rubber mask was placed over his face. Another hand, palm down, pressed on his chest, forcing his lungs to breathe.

Gradually he came out of dying. The lights stopped swimming; the shadows of the men took shape again.

Then, just as he was living, the mask was taken away.

They did it eight, perhaps nine times. Each time was as bad. The knowledge that they would not let him die, that they would revive him in time, was more than cancelled out by the fear that the torture would go on indefinitely.

38

Finally the voice that had first introduced the drug spoke, again clinically.

'I don't expect you to absorb this—you have other things to worry about. But later, perhaps, you might remember. We are not doing this out of cruelty. If we feel it is necessary we can and will modify your behaviour. When you have mistaken ideas we can do this ... when they are right we can reward you.'

He said 'Go ahead' again and again Zorin was forced to die.

At last, when he felt nothing, there was another injection, then spinning, spinning into blackness, and he thanked God for answering his prayer.

There was a bed, made of iron slats, with a mattress and one pillow and blanket. Also a table and stool.

They must have been watching through a peephole. There was hardly time for him to pull himself up before he was being dragged out, along corridors, up in a lift, along more passageways, and finally into the sunlight. Every few seconds Zorin grunted as stabs of pain went through his muscles.

A grey Volga was parked at the kerb.

'This will take you home,' said the major who had first arrested him. Zorin, stumbling, was helped into the back seat. His mind started to function.

'Where is my wife?' His voice rose to a shrill scream. 'Where is she?'

'Please go home. All will be known.'

The car pulled away. Zorin was still sobbing. He realised he was rubbing his wrists raw and swollen from pulling against the bonds.

He looked down at them dumbly for a moment. Then he put his head in his hands and let his whole body shake.

The door had been repaired; otherwise his apartment was as he had left it.

He opened the door and supported himself against the jamb like a drunk.

'Tanya!'

There was no reply. He took hesitant, stumbling steps inside. Papers were strewn over the floor, the mattress lay at an angle, pictures were piled against the walls. His papers and books were still in neat stacks. As far as he could see, they had been returned intact. He stumbled through into the bedroom and sat on the end of the bed. His friends found him there shortly afterwards. They broke the news about Tanya gently.

She had been stripped of her citizenship and deported. Tass had issued a short communiqué, almost a carbon copy of the one issue three weeks before about Solzhenitsyn. But that one had said Solzhenitsyn's wife and children would be allowed to join him.

This report included no such reference.

Sunnenden was a block away from the Russian Embassy, near the Statler, when he considered stopping for a drink. The bar was full of cocktail hour drinkers. Had he spotted an empty table through the gloom he would have stayed. He decided to leave. The previous evening he had denied Janet's gentle criticism that he was drinking more, but it was true. He would have to be careful. He did not have a drinking problem, of course—but Washington was not a town to let anyone get the impression you had.

He walked to the Embassy to gather his thoughts. There had been little time during the day.

It had already been decided that he should attend the Soviet Embassy cocktail party and raise the question of dissidents unofficially once the news had come through about the Zorins. She had been released and deported; she was probably arriving in Israel about now. Of her husband there was no firm news, although unconfirmed intelligence reports said that he was undergoing 'psychiatric treatment'.

That added urgency to his appointment. Sunnenden reminded himself to call Scott later. He would report to him in detail tomorrow, but Scott had asked for at least an indication of how things had gone that evening.

The idea of formally raising the Zorin question with the Soviets had been turned down, either by the Secretary himself or, more likely, by Scott's decision not even to suggest it to his chief.

'It's not the right way, Bob,' he had said. 'We both know that the Ruskies are bound to say "no". So what do we achieve?'

Which was why Sunnenden would raise the question of the Zorins specifically when he arrived at the Embassy.

The cocktail party there was being given in honour of some visiting middle ranking Soviet dignitary. Sunnenden liked to visit the Embassy, which had sparkled under the rule of the Tsars. Now its grim exterior, with shutters almost permanently closed, and its gloomy foyer made it a mysterious place.

As he approached the building Sunnenden saw cars dropping off visitors. Among the parked cars was an unusually large number of Volkswagens—the unofficial staff car of Soviet diplomats below the top rank.

He turned into the circular driveway, large enough for no more than two vehicles. One stood there now, the Soviet Ambassador's Cadillac. The Embassy, grey and heavily covered in ivy, lay less than twenty-five feet from the street. The door was open and Sunnenden joined a straggly queue of visitors having their invitation cards checked.

At the top of the red carpeted stairs was another short queue, this time of people waiting to be presented. The visiting junior minister nodded imperceptibly as Sunnenden was introduced. Sunnenden knew he was being watched. He was not a frequent Embassy party-goer, nor the natural State Department man to be sent to this reception. That he was there for a purpose would be deduced, which would make his task easier.

Sunnenden was not sure what Scott expected to achieve by this approach. He doubted that he could hope to achieve anything more than further confirmation of the Soviets' official attitude about dissidents and a hint about Zorin's whereabouts—which would have no practical benefit. Still, Scott wanted it. 'I've got a feeling, Bob,' he'd said. 'I can't quite finger it, but I think we've got a situation that could turn messy if we don't do something.'

There was vodka and Russian champagne. Sunnenden took the champagne; he disliked it, but he did not trust himself with hard liquor. He worked around the room, occasionally nodding at half-familiar faces, returned the smile of someone he did not recognise, settled himself into a corner.

He caught sight of two Russians he knew. One was an attaché who had once tried, cautiously, to sound him out as a potential spy when he was at Defense. The other was the man with whom Sunnenden hoped to raise the Zorin case.

Khrenin was listed on the mission's list of diplomats as a second secretary, the second lowest ranking. But Sunnenden knew that his position in the Party was considerably higher than those who ostensibly outranked him. What made the charade amusing to Sunnenden was the open deference with which Khrenin's superiors treated him.

He and Sunnenden knew each other. Sipping his drink slowly to make it last, Sunnenden looked up and saw Khrenin watching. The Russian nodded, and moments later the two joined him. Khrenin went through the formality of introducing him to the attaché, who obviously preferred not to recall their previous meeting.

Soon the attaché drifted away. 'You are with the State Department now,' said Khrenin. He had hardly any accent. 'So enormous. Our Foreign Ministry is too big, but compared with the State Department ...' His voice tailed away.

A waiter appeared with a tray of drinks. Sunnenden refused. The Russian took a glass of vodka, drained it in one gulp, replaced the glass and took another.

'I shall probably get drunk,' said the Russian. 'These receptions—so dull. Don't you think so?'

Sunnenden smiled sympathetically but said nothing.

'But, of course, you must, we rarely see you. Wise fellow.'

Again, Khrenin did not wait for a response.

'The State Department,' he continued. 'I'm fascinated. The dear doctor. Such an interesting man. Tell me about him. What is he like to work for? Demanding?'

The Russian's expression now provoked a response, but Sunnenden contented himself with a platitude: 'It's hard work,' he said, 'but worth while.'

That, he thought to himself, was a diplomatic way of stating the truth. Accompanying Dr Kissinger on the Middle East tour had not diminshed his admiration for the Secretary. He *had* been shocked though, to experience Kissinger's personal vanity.

The puritan in Sunnenden recoiled from it. He remembered especially the Secretary's pure delight as he had walked across the lobby of the King David Hotel in Jerusalem while visiting American tourists applauded.

Another waiter appeared. Again Sunnenden refused drinks. The Russian raised his vodka glass.

'They will report me and I will be sent home,' he said laughing. ' "Drinks too much, commits indiscretions with American officials who encourage him to drink and loosen his tongue, while they drink nothing themselves ..." ' He waved a hand at Sunnenden's glass.

Sunnenden suspected the time was not right for more serious talk despite the openings being offered by the Russian. For ten to fifteen minutes he kept the talk general.

He suddenly noticed his glass was empty and, instinctively, glanced at his watch.

Khrenin seized on it. 'Ah, you must leave,' he said, putting an arm around Sunnenden's shoulders. 'Come, I will walk down with you.'

They did not speak again until they were outside. There was no one within earshot. Sunnenden wished he had brought a coat. Perhaps he should go back inside and ask the Embassy to telephone for a cab.

Khrenin led him towards the street. The Russian spoke, as though to himself. 'It is ridiculous, this anti-Soviet feeling,' he said.

Sunnenden forced himself to protest at the statement, but was interrupted. 'No,' Khrenin insisted. 'It is a fact. We both know it. My Ambassador says it is the greatest since Cuba. But why?'

Sunnenden began to answer: Americans were worried about the Middle East, about Vietnam. It was natural ...

They reached the gate.

'You have a car?' asked Khrenin.

'No, I will walk.'

They paused at the gate, both of them knowing that the sparring was over. Khrenin did the prompting: 'You had something to say?'

Sunnenden suddenly felt foolish. 'Zorin. The scientist. The man who has disappeared. His wife was expelled.' Khrenin said nothing. Sunnenden went on. 'You talk about bad feeling. No doubt he's confined somewhere. Freeing him would help.'

There was no expression on Khrenin's face. 'That is your message?'

Sunnenden nodded.

'From the Secretary?'

'I cannot say. But he is concerned.'

Khrenin nodded. Then, again, he put his arm round Sunnenden's shoulders.

'We must keep in touch,' he said. 'Unless of course they take me home and send me to a labour camp for talking to American spies.' He laughed again, then released Sunnenden. 'It would be nice to help. But we cannot. We wish we could, but it would give the wrong impression. This is a time for showing we are strong, not weak. At home as well as overseas. You understand?'

Sunnenden did; the Kremlin hawks were fighting to gain power. The ruling men could not afford to make mistakes.

He was out on the street and Khrenin was saying goodnight. 'But anything else,' the voice called as he moved away, 'anything else, just ask.'

At the Statler, Sunnenden drank two Jack Daniels on the rocks before calling Scott from a pay phone in the lobby. Scott answered immediately.

'No go,' said Sunnenden.

'I thought so,' said Scott. 'Thanks for trying. I'll think some. See you tomorrow.'

There was a click as the line went dead. Sunnenden considered whether he should go to the office, go home, or have a third drink. He was beginning to feel more uneasy than ever.

Scott did little for two days. He read reports of Mrs Zorin's arrival in Israel, and, twenty-four hours later, of the release of her husband after 'hospital treatment'. He listened to Sunnenden's full report of the meeting without comment which pleased, and relieved, Sunnenden. Sunnenden himself had been given a new set of questions to answer on Soviet oil. He had been asked to rewrite the two memoranda on the subject he had already completed.

45

The feeling of being the coming man had diminished. It was as though he had never been singled out. As if he had been found wanting—and not for the first time. On the previous occasion he had been rescued by Scott. What would happen this time?

Scott had other, more pressing problems. A large part of him wanted to forget the Zorin business. Instinct could be wrong. Perhaps he was over-reacting.

Nevertheless, enough belief in his own intuition remained for him to ask Sunnenden to keep a watching brief on the subject. He did it cautiously, knowing that the younger man was feeling touchy about his standing. And he took great care to hint that Sunnenden might later find it worth while. 'If it crops up, Bob,' he said, 'and I'm damned sure it will, the Secretary's going to need someone who really knows what it's all about. There's no one else around.'

Over the following days Sunnenden began collating more information. Zorin and the dissident movement became a minor obsession. Sunnenden began to feel he knew some of them. One thing he could not understand: why did so few try to escape? It would be difficult, of course, but was it impossible? The thought came often.

Less than a week after being given the task by Scott, Sunnenden was rewarded. Scott actually visited his office.

'Better get writing, Bob,' he said. He moved over to an easy chair, forcing Sunnenden to leave his desk and join him.

'All you need to do,' he went on, 'is set down on paper three convincing reasons why the Russian Ambassador should recommend that his government turn friend Zorin loose, and why they should agree.'

'What's happening, and how long have I got?' asked Sunnenden.

Scott stood, his brief visit almost over. 'A lot of people with muscle are leaning on the President. He's got enough problems, so he's leaning on Henry. He sure as hell doesn't like it, but he's got to raise it officially.'

Scott reached the door before seeming to remember there had been two questions. 'Oh, time. I'd say if it was on his desk when he got back from lunch you'd be all right.'

The door closed, and Sunnenden looked at his watch. It was 12.12.

The meeting was a short one. It took place a few minutes before five that afternoon. Sunnenden waited in the anteroom outside Dr Kissinger's seventh-floor office for almost half an hour before he was led in by a secretary.

Kissinger was sitting behind his desk, head inclined to one side, mouth biting on the earpiece of his spectacles. He was reading Sunnenden's memorandum. He did not look up and Sunnenden stood, uncertain whether to sit or cough or even say, 'good afternoon'.

Finally the Secretary looked up. He waved the memorandum towards Sunnenden. 'Would this convince *you*?'

Looking back later Sunnenden was sure he had been right in his reaction: what he was selling was his honest assessment based on his knowledge. He was not a wheeler-dealer like Scott. If he tried to sugar the pill he would get nowhere. He did not have a salesman's personality.

'No,' he said.

The Secretary nodded. 'Nor me.' He picked up a telephone and began dialling. He waved one hand towards Sunnenden who suddenly realised he was being dismissed from the room.

He was stopped near the door by a shout. He turned. 'But a good brief,' said Dr Kissinger. 'A good brief.'

Two days later Scott made up his mind. He did it between telephone calls from his apartment. He glanced at the list of people he still had to reach and decided to leave the rest until morning.

He asked Helen to check whether Sunnenden would be in his office all afternoon. A few minutes later he had the answer: yes.

Soon after, he began the short walk to the State Department building—his second within a week, an event noted with some surprise by the guards on the gate.

The official approach, of course, had had no effect. The Soviet Ambassador said that surely the United States was not attempting to involve itself in the Soviet Union's internal affairs. Were not there far more important matters to concern the two countries?

Scott heard this later the day of the meeting, and would have left the subject alone had it not been for one further event that same evening.

It was after eight. Scott was stretched on a sofa in the Secretary's panelled office, reading *Time* while he waited for Dr Kissinger to finish glancing through papers.

They were going to have dinner, a social evening, a chance for two old friends to exchange thoughts and swap gossip.

'Fuck.' The German accent gave the word added weight.

'What is it?'

Dr Kissinger threw the slim file near Scott's feet. 'The third item,' he said.

The file was one of the twice daily intelligence digests. Item three was a brief report. A highly rated source reported that Mrs Tanya Zorin, in Israel, was pregnant. For the time being the fact was being kept secret.

Scott did not have to ask what the Secretary was thinking: once the news became public a fresh and enormous wave of sympathy and protest would swell. 'I knew we weren't finished with this,' he muttered, half to himself.

Kissinger was not listening. His lower lip was thrust forward—a certain sign of anger. He lifted a pencil and

48

flipped it on to the desk.

'That man was sent to plague me. What madness when the world stands on the edge of war! You'd think *someone* could solve this problem.'

Then, abruptly, he stood.

'Let's go eat.'

It was not a successful evening.

Now, leaving the elevator, Scott found himself reliving some of the same anger. The whole thing was like seeing a lion brought down by bee stings. There were much more important things to consider, not least the fact that the Secretary was due in Moscow by the end of the month.

He turned into the corridor that led to Sunnenden's office, disregarding the wall signs that pleaded with walkers to keep to the right when navigating corners.

Sunnenden was alone. Scott launched straight into what he wanted to say.

'You haven't much on at the moment, have you?'

'Nothing vital.'

'Good.'

He sat on the edge of Sunnenden's desk. Finally he spoke again.

'Remember that crazy thing you said to me when I first asked you to look at the dissidents business?'

'Crazy thing?'

'You said, why don't some of them get out.' Scott turned to stare straight at Sunnenden. 'Well, why don't we help one of them do just that?'

CHAPTER 4

Sunnenden entered the Mayflower Hotel from L Street. Walking through the long, glass-walled lobby with its crystal chandeliers, he imagined that Europe would be like this.

He reached the reception area, jostled with a visiting delegation of Japanese businessmen, turned into the quiet of the Carvery. Cory had spent many years in Europe. Sunnenden wanted to do everything possible to put him in the right frame of mind before he made his proposition.

Cory had not yet arrived, so Sunnenden ordered a drink and debated yet again whether he had been right not to discuss the project with Janet. At first he had not been sure Scott was serious. Was he being tested? For what? Loyalty? His readiness to take a chance? His willingness to use any methods to achieve results?

As they talked, it had become obvious that what Scott was asking was whether there was any way Zorin could be brought out of Russia. Scott made it obvious he did not want to involve himself directly.

'Not that I'm suggesting anyone should do anything silly, Bob,' he said. 'But just think what it would mean if something could be worked out by someone . . .'

After that Sunnenden had called Cory.

His Scotch arrived and he added water carefully. There was no ice in the glass. He was being European.

He sipped, watching the door. On the left an elderly senator he recognised vaguely but could not name was being lobbied by a pretty, intense young woman. 'If I was that someone trying to do something,' Scott had drawled, his eyes smiling, 'I'd get someone who *really* knew the business. And then I'd keep it tight, real tight, until it was all over.'

Sunnenden thought deeply for twenty-four hours, forcing himself not to discuss it with Janet: if anything came of it, he would tell her when it was a success. He kept thinking less about the problem than about the look in Scott's eyes, and his words 'Just think what it would mean . . .' He applied the words to his own future . . .

Finally, he decided that, whatever happened, there was no argument for not taking it one stage further. It was then that he called Cory to suggest this dinner. In the meantime he read Cory's file. The dossier was incomplete and heavily sanitised, but from that and what he already knew he felt he had the right man—if only he would co-operate.

Cory was fifty-four, educated in Europe and England. He was a veteran of the OSS and, in the early days of the CIA, had been with the Office of Policy Co-ordination, a body which used covert intelligence as a cold war weapon. Perhaps its best-known job was setting up Radio Free Europe. From that he had gone back into the field. He was one of the few experienced officers who had not been tainted by the Bay of Pigs.

Soon afterwards he had fallen prey to a surprisingly common intelligence disease: a mental breakdown. The CIA—'the Company'—did everything possible to help him: doctors, long breaks, complete understanding. Within the CIA there is no stigma about mental illness: many Company men are struck and return to duty afterwards as though nothing has happened.

On Sunnenden's left the young woman was reaching over to stroke the senator's hand. She was either taking her job very seriously or Sunnenden had been mistaken.

Cory might easily have returned to the Company too. He was only fifty-two at the time. But he was tired—not of the spy game, but of the new world of faceless, desk-

51

bound bureaucrats who ran it.

It was harder to admit this but Cory also found it increasingly difficult to see the enemy. Once it had been very easy; even during the Cold War it had been 'us' versus 'them'. Now it was so much hazier: on one hand, the Communists were at once the enemy planning to bury the Free World, and the bosom friends of US politicians and businessmen.

Sunnenden saw Cory come through the door and pause. After a few seconds he noticed Sunnenden, but he waited to be led over to the table.

Because of the Middle East trip, Sunnenden had not seen him for over a month. Cory had put on a little weight. Before he had been abnormally thin; now he was simply thin.

He was tall, perhaps six feet six inches, but his round shoulders made him look shorter. His face was lined but not drawn: a map of the past rather than a ravaged victim of it. His short, totally white hair was brushed to one side.

Cory's most striking mannerism was the incline of his head: it leaned slightly to the left, as though he was always on the point of laying it on his left shoulder so that he might doze off. According to some its cause was an old wound; Janet thought it an eccentricity that had become a habit. Whatever the reason, it gave him a perpetually quizzical look.

They shook hands, formally but warmly. When Cory said, 'It's good to see you,' he meant it. He liked the younger man. He found even his faults endearing: Sunnenden's ambition was, to Cory, so blatant that it had a twisted charm. But above all, for a deskbound analyst, Sunnenden had the best understanding of the East–West situation Cory had ever encountered. Sunnenden knew the two blocs had to coexist—and yet he saw the dangers.

They ordered the same main course: prime ribs broiled with peppercorns. Cory declined the invitation to choose the wine but he appreciated the younger man's gesture.

During the meal they touched on many topics: the latest gossip about the President's position, progress in the Ellsburg burglary case, and rumours circulating in State about the health of President Pompidou on the eve of his summit meeting with Brezhnev ... Both men purposely kept the conversation small and light until dessert. If Cory was curious, he showed no sign.

Then Sunnenden looked around. The senator and the girl were leaving. They were walking almost too far apart, as though trying to prove they were near-strangers.

'Would you say this is a safe place to talk?' Sunnenden asked at last.

One of Cory's abilities was to take people as seriously as they would like to be taken. He too looked round theatrically. 'As safe as any, I'd guess—unless you'd like to take a walk.'

Sunnenden spooned a piece of pie, began to raise it and then placed the spoon back on the plate. 'How easy would it be to get a man out of Moscow?'

'Does he want to go?'

'That's assumed.'

'Is he at all well known?'

Sunnenden nodded.

Cory leaned across the table. 'You're serious?'

'Yes,' said Sunnenden. Suddenly the other's reaction had made it all very real.

Cory leaned back again. 'Then I think I'll have second thoughts on what I said earlier. We might have to take that walk after all.'

But they did not walk. Instead they drove in Sunnenden's Ford along the Potomac, found a parking area, and doused the lights.

Only then did Sunnenden return to the subject. 'It's serious enough. We want to know if it could work. That's why we need your help.'

53

'*We?* Is it official?' Cory knew it could not be—he would not have been approached in this way. Still, he wanted to know the ground rules from the start.

Sunnenden paused. One of the first questions he had asked himself when the subject was raised was Why us? Why not go talk to the CIA? They're paid for this kind of thing. Sunnenden had debated asking Scott the same question. But he already knew the answer. The CIA was going through a difficult period. Vietnam, Watergate, and détente had each dealt its blows; Bill Colby, its director since the previous July, was being pressured to phase out much of the agency's covert side. Scott would reckon the only way to get official CIA help on a project like this was for Kissinger to give a direct order. Too risky if things went wrong.

'Yes, we,' said Sunnenden. 'But not official. If anything went wrong, our principals would not like to be embarrassed.'

Cory smiled to himself : 'Principals'—Sunnenden had even researched the jargon!

Sunnenden paused, wondering if that was enough. Cory said nothing. Obviously it was not. 'All I can say is that it goes up high, very high.'

So, thought Cory, did Watergate. 'All right,' he said. 'Tell me how it is, the bare details first.'

After the brief outline Sunnenden was asked to tell the story again, this time elaborating as much as he wished. From time to time Cory interrupted with a question.

When Sunnenden had finished, Cory leaned forward, his chin supported in his hands. 'You say it would be unofficial. But could we get help?'

'Some,' replied Sunnenden. 'But of course it would be best to keep it to a minimum.' He paused. 'You've got good contacts . . .'

It was more a statement than a question, but Cory decided to disregard the point. 'Let's go, shall we?'

For the whole journey to Georgetown Cory sat in the same bent position. When the car stopped he didn't move. Sunnenden broke the silence. Anything that was to be said had to be raised now.

'Well,' he asked, 'could it be done?'

'I don't know,' said Cory. He opened the door and started to slide out.

'I'll think a while and call you,' he said. Then very formally, 'And thank you for a pleasant evening. Tell Janet I missed her.'

At the door Cory paused, caught for a few seconds in the Ford's lights as Sunnenden turned in the road. It was a big house, too big for one man. At regular intervals realtors wrote, telephoned or even called in person to suggest he sell it. None of them seemed to understand that he neither needed nor wanted the money.

He did want the house. For years, living in the field, he had worked out of a suitcase. When he returned to the house left to him by an aunt, he had embarked on an orgy of collecting. Apart from the sculpture, there had been secondhand books, wine, and objects impossible to categorise—anything that caught his fancy, from an old horn gramophone that sat next to the hi-fi to a set of Degas lithographs that he had given himself the day he decided he had finally come through the breakdown.

Friends said Cory wore his wealth like an old slipper. Never having been without money, he took its existence for granted. Until his return he had spent little of it. He continued to increase his fortune not from diligence or financial brilliance, but from a number of relatives, all moderately rich and childless, who seemed to take it in turns to die and leave him yet another legacy.

Cory removed his raincoat, kicked off his shoes and settled back into a deep leather chair, his feet raised on a leather footstool in front. Without moving from the chair,

55

he reached over and turned on the tape-recorder. Telemann filled the room. Then, from the table at his side, he poured Armagnac from a decanter, sipped—and began to think.

He had to confess that he liked the idea of bringing someone out of Moscow.

A major reason for his quitting the CIA was that he had feared the possibility of being shunted off to some sinecure, to ride the desk as so many other career men did, until the day of retirement. What he liked about espionage was precisely the kind of problem and challenge that lay before him now.

And then, of course, there was Sunnenden. He felt he owed the younger man something for preventing him from vegetating. It was Sunnenden who had persuaded him to return to government as a part-time consultant. They had met while Sunnenden was at Defense. Cory was detailed to brief him on some Soviet 'advisers' who were active in Chile. Sunnenden had been impressed by the man's knowledge and approach.

They met again after Cory's illness, at an exhibition of Eskimo sculpture. It was one of Janet's passions and one, it emerged, of Cory's. A loose friendship developed. After moving to State Sunnenden propositioned the Department about a job that he thought ought to be created: they needed someone with immense background knowledge to sift reports of Soviet intentions and assess whether or not they were genuine.

Cory closed his eyes, remembering Moscow. Images unrolled like a film track. He walked across Red Square on the coldest day of the year; he huddled in a taxi, talking with the old woman driver in bad Russian, breathing that mixture of smells found nowhere else—sweat and garlic and rough tobacco; he fumbled under a bench and removed a small metal container ... His thoughts began to drift. He sipped and fell into a light sleep. Pictures, pleasant ones, flashed through his mind. Then there was another: the twisted car, a severed arm, a smell of blood in his nostrils. And then Sue's face. For a second he felt it all again.

He pulled himself up, his head pounding. The tape had finished. He poured more brandy and drank quickly, breathing deeply. It was all right. He checked all the alarms and went to bed.

Cory had intended to go back on to valium the following morning—just to be on the safe side. It had been months since the vision had returned. But he felt too good to bother. He was working and the problem fascinated him. He needed to work; he needed this kind of challenge to stretch him and test him and make him feel fully alive again. He looked down at his hands: when he was with other people, he could control them. Alone, his fingers shook. Today, for the first time for months, they were steady.

Cory ate breakfast in the small bay-windowed room overlooking the street. It was a remarkably small room—large enough for a dining table and, at most, three chairs—yet it enjoyed a prime position in the house. He had never understood what quirk in the original owner or designer had made them build it that way.

By the side of the plate he had a Russian guidebook open to a map of the city. He kept looking at it as though this would give him the inspiration he needed to solve Sunnenden's problem.

There were actually two problems to be solved. The first was the straight mechanics of moving a person out of the country; the second was covering the man's absence from his home and usual haunts while you did it.

The simplest solution to the second problem might be to have the man taken ill. But before he knew if that would work he would need answers to many questions: How

57

closely did the KGB watch? If Zorin was apparently confined to bed, would they call? Would a doctor be summoned—and if so, who?

Cory poured more coffee from the jug on the electric tray. He dunked a piece of roll, splashing coffee on to the plain oak surface.

Move him out as baggage or as a person? By rail, road, air, sea, or on foot?

Cory had never before tried to get anyone out of Russia. East Germany, yes, and once out of Poland. But he had been on the spot and there had been routes. Compared to Russia, they were easy.

Cory poured the rest of the coffee into his cup and carried it into his work room. Despite the elaborate alarms that guarded the house, he kept the door locked. Inside, a dark mahogany table ran over half the length of the room. The table was covered with books and papers; the piles looked haphazard, but Cory knew what every one contained. He cleared a space on the table and proceeded to fill it with books he took from his shelves: guides, timetables...

He read until 12.30, when he walked down to Martin's Tavern for some fried scallops and two glasses of beer.

He worked through the whole afternoon and much of the evening. He finished reading just after 2 a.m., was up again before seven, and an hour later was on his way to Langley. Apart from his State Department assignment and his thirty years of contacts, Cory held consultancy status with the CIA. Two, perhaps three times a month he would travel out to talk, to give his opinion on documents, or an outside evaluation of how an operation was looking. Today the visit was at Cory's request. There were files he needed to examine. He had added to his requisition list a number of files he did not need—hopefully no pattern would show.

He spent the day reading through files on dissidents,

Zorin especially, on internal security in Russia—particularly at sea and at airports—and on Soviet documentation. He left late that night, handing his badge and key to the night security officer. He sat in the back of the car, his eyes closed, his mind reeling with a kaleidoscope of facts.

Five days after first raising the subject of Zorin with Cory, Sunnenden was outside his home in Chevy Chase playing at being a gardener. He enjoyed prowling around the lawns, prodding the odd flower bed with a rake, happy in the knowledge that a professional gardener saw to the real work. It was nearly eleven o'clock, the time he had suggested Cory arrive. It would give them time to talk alone—and without risk of being overheard—in the rambling garden before the other guests arrived for brunch.

In the previous five days Sunnenden had seen Cory only once. Cory asked him a long series of questions, refusing to answer any himself. 'I still need to know more,' he had explained.

One thing he had said, chilled Sunnenden, particularly coming as it did in Cory's gentle monotone: 'Are you sure you need your man somewhere other than Russia? Or could he just not be there?'

It had taken more than a moment for Sunnenden to understand. 'You mean . . . ?'

'I mean,' said Cory, 'that if your man is just an embarrassment where he is, there are easier ways of dealing with that than getting him out.'

'No, we need him out.'

'Fine. But it had to be discussed.'

Cory was late. It was 11.20 when the cab turned into the drive of Sunnenden's house. Janet insisted they have coffee before Sunnenden led Cory on a tour of the garden.

'Too cold?' asked Sunnenden. Cory was wearing a

turtleneck sweater and a tweed sports jacket, but there was a damp chill in the air.

'No, it's all right, and I think we should talk. That is, if you're still serious.'

Twenty-four hours earlier Sunnenden would not have been sure. Nothing new had emerged. He and Scott had met once, but the subject had not been raised, even in Scott's oblique way.

Then had come fresh reports from the White House: they too were worried about the latest news from Israel. Obviously the pressures were not going to ease. 'I sure hope someone somewhere is doing something,' Scott had said to Sunnenden. 'He'd make a lot of people very happy and do himself a heap of good.' And Sunnenden made his decision.

'Yes,' he said to Cory. 'We're serious, about as serious as you can get.'

He stopped by the swing the boys had used when they were younger. He bent and pushed the seat.

'In fact,' he confided, 'I'm under some pressure to get something moving.'

The two began to walk, Cory with his hands clasped behind his back. He looked exhausted. 'Let me tell you the way it is, then. If your principals want to go into this they ought to know the problems they face. Agree?'

Sunnenden did.

'All right,' said Cory. 'The Soviets spend a lot of money, manpower and expertise keeping people in as well as out—and they are pretty good at it. You can't even move from one part of the country to another without their knowing. To get into an airport or on to a train you need papers. If the informers didn't pick you out, there's five hundred detectives on watch duty at airports alone.'

They stopped and Sunnenden picked up a tennis ball from the thick grass. He tossed it from hand to hand.

'I'm following,' he said. It was basic stuff, but Cory

obviously wanted to tell it from the beginning.

Cory rubbed his face with both hands and continued. 'I've checked out your man as much as I can without arousing suspicions. He's under twenty-four-hour surveillance. Fortunately he's been keeping a low profile so at the moment he's not being bothered much.

'If he goes out for a walk, they note the time he leaves and then someone follows him. When he gets back, they check him in. And they keep an overnight watch. Incidentally, I hope you've made damn sure he *wants* to come out ... Theoretically he might creep out then under cover of dark, but he'd have to pass frighteningly near their car —and apart from the *upravdom* we don't know who else they might have in the block.'

Sunnenden was still tossing the ball from hand to hand. 'Could he shake off his tail during the day?'

'Oh yes, no problem. Sometimes there's only one, mostly there's two, and that's no way to keep a man in view if he wants to shake you. But what happens then? Out goes the alarm that your man is missing. I doubt they would think he was trying to get out of the country if that happened—the watch seems to be to isolate him from other dissidents and Western journalists. But as a matter of routine the alert would include railway terminals, air and sea ports, highway police and border guards. I wouldn't give much for his chances of staying loose for more than a few hours, let alone getting out of the country.'

'It sounds pretty gloomy.'

The two men were still facing each other. Sunnenden threw the ball to the ground.

Cory's voice was so low that Sunnenden had to strain to hear him.

'I thought I should tell you the way it is. You know your Soviets, but I don't think you really appreciate what a marvellous machine they've got for repression.' He raised his hand. 'Oh yes, you know in theory. But I'm telling you what it means in practice if you're to get your man out.' He smiled, an indication that the admonition was over. After a long pause, he went on.

'What I've outlined is only the first of the problems to be faced. We've still got to move him. I thought of all the normal ways of smuggling him out—across the Black Sea to Turkey, on to a seagoing boat at Leningrad—but I think they're too damned risky. I even toyed with the idea of hijacking a plane. But I guess he'd need some help, and I wouldn't like to do it that way. Remember the last people who tried?'

Sunnenden nodded. The twelve people who attempted to hijack a plane for Leningrad to Sweden . . .

'I played around with concealing him on a train or in a car to cross one of the border points. The best place would be something like Vyborg into Finland. But if you've ever crossed that border and seen the way they've stripped the land bare, the way they go through things . . .'

He became quiet and Sunnenden wondered whether he was remembering something specific that had happened to him.

'No,' said Cory suddenly. 'I'd reckon the odds are too much in their favour.'

'But it can be done?' Sunnenden demanded. 'You have an idea?'

Cory caught the impatience in Sunnenden's voice. 'Yes,' he said. 'I think so.' He turned to face Sunnenden so that he could watch his reaction. 'We can't bring him out as Zorin,' he said. 'All right then. *We'll turn him into someone else!*'

On the slow walk back in the direction of the house Sunnenden fired questions, his speech more clipped than ever, his arms waving oratorically as he introduced each new query.

Twice his voice was punctuated by Janet calling to them that brunch guests had arrived.

Cory let the younger man exhaust his questions before beginning his replies.

'All right, all right,' he said. 'The way I see it is that the only chance of making this work is bringing our friend out as a foreigner returning home. That way the checks are minimal.'

'But won't their routine records show that whoever he's pretending to be never arrived in Russia?' interrupted Sunnenden. 'Don't they keep files on things like that?'

'Oh yes. That's the beauty of it, I think.' Cory was smiling now. They were nearing the house.

'You see, in the first place we send someone in. He changes places with Zorin, and *he's* the man the KGB are watching while Zorin gets out.'

The two men came in sight of the drive. Sunnenden saw the two-tone Buick: his sister and her husband. A jumbled succession of questions was in his mind. 'But won't this other man need to be a double for Zorin?' he asked.

'Only passably like him to start. We can do the rest.'

'Then he's the one stuck in Moscow. How do we get *him* out?' Then with a rare hint of humour, he added: 'Send in another double?'

'A slight problem but nothing compared with getting out a well-known Russian dissident.'

They paused a few yards from the house. Sunnenden had a lot he wanted to ask but knew that unless he went inside, one of the boys would be sent out to fetch them. The discussion could come later—but there was one question he had to ask now.

'How do we find this man?'

'Now that,' said Cory, beckoning the younger man to lead the way to the door, 'really *is* the problem.'

CHAPTER 5

It was late afternoon before Sunnenden and Cory were able to talk again. Around 3.30 the party started to break up. Sunnenden offered to drive Cory home, hinting to Janet that he needed to pick up some papers anyway.

Not for the first time Janet wondered why there had been such an abrupt change in her husband's mood. Before his return from the Middle East everything had been going well; then he had become subdued—his mood not far removed from a time months before when he had made what could have been a damaging mistake. But this time she knew of nothing. And now he had about him this preoccupied almost conspiratorial air.

What was both strange and worrying was Sunnenden's unwillingness to discuss it with her. One of the great strengths of their relationship was that they had always talked about everything. She also knew, as she had always known, that her husband needed her resolve to bring out that little extra bit in him. This time she had forced herself to wait for him to volunteer what was happening. She had been reluctant to ask but now, as the house emptied, she decided that later she would.

Cory and Sunnenden made small talk in the car. Cory wanted to be in his own surroundings before continuing, and Sunnenden felt reluctant to ask questions in case the whole scheme was falling apart.

They moved into the lounge and, without asking, Cory poured brandies. Then he excused himself, returning a few minutes later with a small pile of papers.

'All right,' he said, as they both sat, 'now let's pull the whole idea apart.'

This was the moment in preliminary planning that every intelligence officer both loves and dreads—the moment when the idea becomes real, when it makes sense enough to discuss. The fear, of course, is that it won't stand scrutiny, that an unknown or forgotten factor will emerge and negate everything.

'Before we go on, let me just make sure I've got the idea?' Sunnenden put down his drink, still untouched, and held out his left hand, ticking off points on his fingers as he made them. 'One, we send in someone who looks enough like Zorin to exchange places with him. Two, somehow they make the switch. And three, the Russian comes out using the American's papers. Right?'

Cory nodded. Stated baldly like that, it sounded unlikely but not ridiculous.

'Okay,' continued Sunnenden, brisk now, slipping into his role as prosecuting attorney, 'let's leave aside the two big ones for now—how we find this man and then how we get him out. How much like the subject would he have to look?'

Cory sorted through the papers he had on his lap. He found the photographs he wanted and handed them to Sunnenden.

'That's your man,' he said.

Sunnenden put on his spectacles. He knew the face: not only was it familiar from newspapers, but he had seen a score of photographs of it since he had first been asked to prepare a brief on dissidents. These pictures, though, were different angles, different distances. In facial close-ups virtually every pore showed.

'Taken during an ordinary press conference photo-session,' explained Cory. 'Fairly routine for someone like that if you've access and a friendly newspaper photographer around.' He did not add that in the early days of

Zorin's civil rights agitation the CIA had investigated the possibility that he might be a 'plant'. He had been cleared of suspicion, but the files remained. 'They're two years old, good enough for our purpose initially.'

Cory handed over a sheet of paper. 'You only need glance at it, but those are your man's statistics as up to date as I could get them.'

Sunnenden took in the main ones: height, 5 ft 11 in; weight 171 pounds; hair dark, beard flecked with grey; eyes blue-grey...

'All right,' Cory went on, 'we have to take the chance that our American—let's call him Smith—is not going to be picked up while he's pretending to be Zorin. If he is, he's just dead. What we need then is someone who up to a few feet away outside, dressed up, looks and moves enough like him.

'We need somone of the right height and build. That's the basic. It would be nice if we got things like the eyes right, but we can use contact lenses if we have to. The complexion can be fixed, and Zorin's got this lovely beard...'

Cory produced a sketchpad from his pile of papers. 'Now look at this.' He left Sunnenden staring at the first page while he poured more brandy. On the page were two pen drawings, both of faces full-on. The one on the right was obviously Zorin. Cory handed Sunnenden the re-plenished glass and swirled his own. 'As you see,' he said, 'Zorin on the right. The one on the left is Mr Smith.'

The sketch of Zorin was faithful, but drawn in the style of a cartoon—picking out the main features of the Russian's face. The other drawing consisted of no more than the outline of the head, a nose the same shape as Zorin's, the shape of cheekbones, eyes, mouth, and ears.

'All right, turn it over.'

Sunneden turned the page. The next pair of drawings

66

was identical except that Smith's hair had been cut and shaded darker.

In the next pair Smith had a beard. Gradually the two pictures became the same.

'Keep turning.'

'It looks all right.' Sunnenden looked cautiously up. 'But we're back to finding the right man.'

'Right. But we need less than you'd suppose. I went to see an old contact in New York, someone who used to be out on the Coast with Disney. He's a makeup man the Company uses from time to time. He's retired now. An old timer like me.' Cory smiled.

While talking, Cory had been riffling through the papers. He found the sheet he wanted.

'These are the essentials. He needs to be about the right height—it doesn't matter if he's a bit smaller, we can build him up. Same with the weight, though here he could be heavier and we could slim him down. Fortunately the beard disguises some of the things that could be a problem —like the chin. The nose is pretty important, but a bit can be done to pad it out. Zorin's ears are fairly normal. He's got a prominent gold tooth that shows, but we could get a dentist to work on Smith; he wouldn't even have to know what it was about. Given a few things, we can add the rest ourselves.'

'What about the language?'

'Ideally, yes. I'd like it. I guess it might work without it, but I'd be extra nervous. One important thing we've got going for us is that Zorin's got good English and like a lot of those academics speaks it with an American accent of sorts.'

'All right,' said Sunnenden. 'Let's suppose for now that Smith can be turned into Zorin. Won't we need experts out there to do it after he arrives?'

'That worried me. But my New York contact reckons it could be done quickly and easily on the spot by Smith

67

himself. We would have to prepare Smith's change as much as we could in advance.'

He leaned over Sunnenden's chair and turned the pages of the sketchpad until he came to the picture he wanted.

'Take the gold teeth,' he said. 'That's obviously taken care of. But we don't want Smith going into Moscow with it showing all over the place, so it's loosely capped. It can be fixed to be just yanked off. Smith would have to be careful biting while he'd got it on, but that's all.

'Same with the hair. New York figures dye and cut it here and send Smith in with a wig over it. Then all he needs do is take off the wig.'

It was dark outside, and Cory walked across to the window to work the drapes. Then, as though sensing Sunnenden's scepticism, he added, 'It sounds a little crazy, I know, but the more I've thought about turning Smith into Zorin the less mad it seems.'

'Yes, but you've got to change Zorin into Smith too.' It was strange: until that moment he had not thought of this part of the problem.

Cory smiled. He had obviously been waiting with relish for this question.

'Example,' he said. 'Smith goes in wearing a wig to disguise the fact that he's had his hair cut and dyed to look like Zorin's. Question: What does Zorin do to look like Smith when the moment comes?'

'He puts on an identical wig.'

'Right. And if Smith takes off a white cap to expose a gold tooth, what does Zorin do to hide his?'

Sunnenden was smiling now. 'Your New York man thinks it could work?'

'He does. We can repeat these things right across the board. Give Smith glasses, he takes them off when he wants to start transforming himself into Zorin, Zorin puts on a pair . . .

'My New York contact says we can have one other thing going for us. We give Smith a few characteristics that Zorin can adopt when the times comes. When most men look at other people they focus in on one thing. Zorin's got his beard. We might give Smith a scar, or a funny way of walking. A limp would be an easy one. Something Zorin could adopt quickly and people would notice.'

A grandfather clock in the hallway began to chime. 'Six,' said Cory. 'I don't want to get rid of you, but perhaps you shouldn't leave Janet much longer.' He paused to see if there was a reaction. There was not. 'You haven't said anything to her?'

'No, I wondered whether I should, but decided against it.'

'She knows something is happening?' Cory had sensed it at brunch. 'I would tell her something—not the truth, but something that sounds convincing. It will make life easier for both of you. You've got yourself into a business where you'll find that the odd lie makes life bearable.' He stared down at his glass and Sunnenden got the feeling that the older man was remembering something quite specific.

The meeting finished soon after that. They agreed that the next step was for Cory to find the right man.

Only after Sunnenden had gone did Cory realise just how tired he was. Almost too tired to eat, he thought. The week's newspapers and magazines were still piled on a table in the hallway. He picked up a bundle and carried them to his bedroom. It was a surprisingly feminine room: patterned wallpaper, soft lighting, a double bed with a cane headboard and, by the side of the dressing-table mirror, the only memento he had allowed himself to keep, a small watercolour of Sue painted by an artist friend.

Looking at it and remembering—but just a little—was a nightly ritual.

In the morning Cory called Denton and arranged a meeting for noon.

Like Sunnenden, Cory's first feeling about the substitute for Zorin had been that physical characteristics were the most crucial factor. Now he realised that, although these remained important, there were other vital ones: the man's willingness to be involved, and his ability to function under the kind of stress that he would face.

The man could not be an intelligence officer: his capture—and that was a possibility—would be too embarrassing. At the same time, Cory could hardly approach strangers for the job. The answer, if there was one, was probably already on file.

No one—himself included—could do anything other than guess at the number of Americans whose secrets were on file with government bodies, credit services, detective agencies, and in the records of private companies. Cory would push as many buttons as possible, getting the computers to spill out the information on anyone who satisfied his basic requirements.

On those computerised files there would be hundreds, perhaps even thousands, who might be worthy of further checks. But in practice Cory's actions were restricted by the way the files were organised.

He had worked out and listed what he sought: the man's size and age limits, race, facial characteristics. Then he added others which would make the subject even more desirable: first, knowledge of Russian, then single status...

Five government computer files were possible sources, but he discounted three: these were the ones kept by the Treasury, the Department of Health, Education and Welfare, and the CIA. Domestic names on the CIA's records

70

would be people they had used or men judged politically suspect; neither group was suitable for such an assignment into Russia. HEW's would also cover people who were suspect politically, though only in the fields the Department covered. The Treasury files were extensive—nine sets in fact, including those of Internal Revenue Intelligence and the Secret Service. But Cory thought it unlikely he would find the man he wanted among such figures as suspected tax avoiders and potential assassins.

The fourth was Defense, and that was a possibility. The one he favoured most was the fifth—the FBI's. The men recorded on this computer would be known criminals. Where better to look for a man who might be persuaded to undertake such a mission—in return, of course, for money? And such a man might well have the right psychological makeup. The use of a criminal would be nothing new in the intelligence world.

The second reason was that Cory knew someone with access to this computer: Denton, a friend since wartime. And with this, as with everything else that might be involved, Cory wanted to work at an unofficial level, using the old buddies system as much as possible.

Denton was with the FBI's computer system, the National Crime Information Center.

Cory took a cab to the Justice Department. One of the young FBI men on escort duty confirmed that he was expected and took him to Denton's office.

Cory had not seen Denton in over a year, but they shared a friendship that did not depend on regular meetings.

For the past year Denton's main role at the FBI, as Cory recalled it, was selling the network to the public and the Congress, and trying to persuade both that the computer was not a foretaste of a 1984-ish America.

Cory was ushered into Denton's office. They shook

71

hands and Denton smiled: a king among smiles, combining as it did genuine pleasure and his months of practice of public relations for the NCIC network.

'You'll stay around for lunch?' asked Denton.

'If you're free, I'd love to.'

'Fine. Then if it's okay with you, I'll launch right away into my computer spiel and save up everything I want to ask you till then.'

Cory listened intently as Denton explained the system's history: it was, said Denton, essentially just a huge automated file cabinet. Here in the FBI were eight of those automated files, computer storage units holding local, state and federal information on wanted persons and stolen property.

Cory found his attention wandering: his eyes tried to take in the room without reflecting his growing boredom with what was obviously a prepared speech meant to cover everyone from visiting schoolchildren to politicians.

He found himself wondering how Denton could tolerate the job, let alone enjoy it, as he apparently did. Denton had had a lot of field posts before returning to Washington where, at one time, it was rumoured that he was even a possibility to take over when the Old Man went. Now, to Cory's mind, his job was no more than riding out the few years to retirement. The NCIC job was one Cory would have regarded as an insult, and to see Denton in it saddened him.

The lecture went on: 140,000 transactions a day, six thousand terminals throughout the country in police departments and sheriffs' offices and state police facilities ...

Denton drained his coffee, and put down his cup. Then he gave a broad smile. 'Oh shit,' he said, 'I don't know why I'm giving you all this. I'm so programmed that you just say "tell me about NCIC" and I give you the whole commentary.

'Instead, come on,' he said, starting to move, 'let me

72

show you how it works. That's what you want.'

It was so smoothly done that Cory wondered whether even this wasn't rehearsed, like the singer's reluctant encore or the good politician's impromptu speech. Denton checked his watch as they passed though the door. It was 12.10. The tour was obviously on schedule.

The computer room was on the same floor. Cory was surprised by it after Denton's buildup. It was much smaller scale than he had thought: he had imagined a vast complex like the control room in a Bond film. As it was there were four terminals, resembling a cross-breed of electric typewriters with news agency wire machines. Operatives sat behind only two of them. The only indication that the room was in the FBI building was the posters on the walls for the ten most wanted men.

Denton paused by one of the manned machines and introduced Cory. Cory nodded atentively as working details were spelled out. He waited for a pause and then asked, 'What about the CCH files?' He hoped he had remembered the name rightly.

He had. 'Sure, I'd meant to talk about that next,' said Denton. The Computerised Criminal History file had been added to the computer in November 1971, he explained. Basically it comprised the records of men and women convicted of serious crimes, either federal or in the half dozen states participating in this part of the project.

'At this stage,' Denton said in a confiding tone, 'I'd normally explain to you why the existence of these files is a protection of people's freedom, not a threat as some nutty radicals insist. I'd tell you that all these details were available manually before and that all we've done is to make them easier to use. But'—and there was another smile—'I'm taking it we're on the same side . . .'

Cory was surprised to find himself responding unfavourably. The pitch was so strong that he felt himself thinking: Oh yes, and what about military, and Secret Service, and prison and postal inspection and whatever other details are filed away in your same computer? He knew from other sources that they were there. He remained silent.

'Okay,' said Denton, 'let's give you a run-through.' And then, as though Cory were not present, he added, 'Sid, can you give me a CCH?'

'Sure thing, Mr Denton.'

The operative began tapping out keys. They leaned over and watched.'

'This is a phoney record, one we keep for testing and demonstration,' explained Denton. 'Sidney is asking what they've got on a man whose name we don't know but whose army number we've got.'

Within seconds the machine began printing its reply. Denton held the top straight so they could read it as it came out. The whole message ran to about fifty lines, full of abbreviations. Denton explained them: on the input QH meant it was an inquiry for a man's criminal history; a row of letters beginning DCH was the computer's acknowledgement.

'All we've asked for is a summary,' he said. 'If we want the full record we'll ask again.'

Cory followed the sheet down as Denton translated. The reply began with the detail that the subject was 'multiple state': he had committed crimes in more than one state. It gave his FBI file number, date of birth, name, height, colour of eyes, hair. Denton was tracing the lines with his finger. It stopped at 'SMT'—'That means scars, marks, tattoos,' he said. The reply went on to give aliases, arrests, convictions and all identifying marks and characteristics.

'Here.' Denton tore off the strip. 'Keep it as a souvenir.'

He checked his watch again. 'Let's try some lunch,' he said.

It was just 12.30. Another tour was over, on schedule.

Denton had booked a table at Hammel's, a favourite spot for the Justice Department.

The room was noisy and crowded enough for them both to feel anonymous. Denton seemed different away from his office.

'Do you miss it, Jim?' he asked.

'The job?'

'Yes.'

Both men stared down at the table, remembering.

They first met in the war; friendship had been forged in strength in the late fifties when both had been operating in London. Denton was at one of the FBI's overseas 'liaison bureaux', set up by J. Edgar Hoover ostensibly to allow continuous contact with foreign police forces for the exchange of information. In reality, their work went into the world of espionage.

In London, Denton found no problem getting full co-operation from Scotland Yard's Special Branch, nor from MI5. It was different, though, when it came to the British Secret Service; that organisation preferred to deal only with officers of its direct counterpart, the CIA. That meant Cory. He, in turn, needed Denton's contacts. The two men rapidly developed an excellent working relationship that blossomed into friendship.

Cory was the first to raise his eyes. His voice was full of meaning. 'I keep my hand in.'

'So I heard.'

Halfway through the meal Denton asked the question he had been keeping back ever since Cory phoned him that morning.

'Are you back with it, Jim? Is that what this is all about?'

'May I ask you one question? About that computer of yours?'

'Sure. As long as you don't think you're getting out of answering mine.'

Cory knew the answer, but wanted it confirmed. He also wanted Denton's reaction. 'That last summary record you got from the computer, you got it in response to feeding in an army number.'

Denton nodded agreement.

'And you could have got it from feeding in a full name?' Cory continued. 'Or an FBI file number? Or a prison number? Or a social security number?'

Denton kept nodding.

'What if you'd done it all backwards—fed in details like height and age and all that? Would it have worked?'

Denton did not have to think. 'Officially, no. That's the kind of thing that scares people, the Big Brother bit I was talking about. But between us, yes. You wouldn't get just one guy, of course—you'd get everybody who fitted those details you fed in.'

There was a long pause while plates were cleared, dessert and coffee ordered, and while Denton fought with his vow not to smoke before 6 p.m. and lost.

'Now my question,' he said at last.

'Let me answer it with a question.'

'Another?'

They were both enjoying it. This was the way it used to be.

'Can you work the computer?'

Denton nodded. 'Sure, there's no more to it than working a typewriter once you know the call symbols.'

'Suppose,' Cory said, 'that I came to you with the kind of details I've mentioned and asked you to feed them in and see what names came out. What would you say?'

'You're looking for someone?'

'That's right.'

'And you don't know his name or anything, but suspect he's got a record. Right?'

'Right.'

Denton took a packet of Sweet 'N Low from the bowl, tore the end and poured half carefully into his coffee. 'Who would it be for?'

'Our side. But it has to be unofficial. That's all I can say.'

'You can't make a straight request?'

'My people are trying to avoid it.'

The answer came surprisingly quickly. Denton downed his coffee in a gulp, signalled for more, and said briskly, 'Okay, why not? You give me the detail, I'll do it one evening when there's only one operative on. I'll tell him I'll sit watch an hour so why doesn't he go and get a drink...'

He felt Cory's eyes questioning him. His voice became slower, his tone more explanatory. 'Jim,' he began hesitantly, 'I know what you and lots of others must think about this damn job I've got now.' He raised his hand to forestall any denial. 'Okay, it's comfortable, but it's a shit-eating job. That's why all the bright spiel.' He paused and Cory waited, not wanting to interrupt. 'Christ, Jim, what I'm saying is that it's so damn boring. I'd do almost anything just to get my heart pounding again the way it used to. Even digging out files after everyone's gone home ...'

The coffee came and he poured in the rest of the sweetener. 'I've got fifteen more months and then I retire. To do what? Let's just say you want it and that's good enough for me.'

Fifteen minutes later they said goodbye. Cory slipped him the note listing the details; Denton promised to try to use the computer within the next two days.

Denton suddenly seemed to remember all he had to do. He checked his watch, became brisk, said how good it had been and that he would call, and then turned away. Cory called after him.

'One thing, just a small one. I forgot to ask.'

'Yes?' Denton was making no secret of the fact that he was late.

Cory suddenly thought better of it. 'No, it's all right. I'll ask you when we talk.'

He was glad he had stopped himself. It was good that Denton was willing to co-operate this far. He would ask him later how easy it was to destroy a man's record on the files so that to all intents and purposes the man had never existed.

CHAPTER 6

There were twenty-nine sheets of paper from Denton, all six inches wide, eighteen inches long, and all printed in capital letters. After the first half dozen Cory found himself reading the computer's abbreviations without effort: blu he knew was blue, bron was brown, UR was upper right arm, DLU meant the date the file was last updated.

After several careful readings, Cory discounted eight for varying reasons. One man had a pronounced facial scar, another had a finger missing, three had histories of narcotics use . . .

Cory divided the twenty-one files remaining into three piles: the possibles, the interesting, and the very interesting. One of the files in the interesting list was only placed there after much thought: the man seemed perfect except for one disturbing fact.

Seated in his study, much of the table now cleared by the expedient of moving some piles of books on to the floor, Cory juggled the file in his mind. He was uncertain whether to discard it altogether or place it in the very interesting stack. Finally he compromised; he would decide later.

The next stage worried him. He now needed to examine the men's full records, including psychiatric reports. This full detail, he knew, was not on computer. He needed more co-operation from Denton.

Denton accepted the request as a pure logistics problem. The files, he thought, should be removed from the building a few at a time. The chance of anyone wanting to see them while they were missing was several million to one, but Cory rented a hotel room near by so that the files could be delivered, read, and returned within two hours.

The first batch consisted of five files. Cory found that reading and making notes took him longer than he had anticipated. The following morning he bought a small copier machine and moved it to his room in a suitcase. From then on it was easier. He would skim a page and if it looked interesting copy it. After four days he checked out, paying in cash.

The next time that he sorted his files there were eleven in the discard pile, leaving only ten. Cory decided five of these were possibles, three were interesting, and one was very interesting. That left one over—the one that had worried him from the start. This man seemed to be ideal; he even had Russian. But the one problem fact remained...

Using two fingers, he typed up basic details on all ten and attached the sheets to the original FBI computer tear-offs. The rest of the papers he placed in his safe. He would have been happier destroying them, but he needed to keep them until a decision was made. He did, however, remove the electric typewriter ribbon and put it on one side to be burned.

Only then did he call Sunnenden and suggest a meeting. It was a brief one, even though Sunnenden had been pressing him for information for days. Sunnenden read the files, nodded a few times, but asked no questions. Finally he asked whether he could keep the papers for a day.

They were sitting in Sunnenden's car. Cory had been invited home for drinks. They had pulled off the road for Sunnenden to examine the papers.

Cory had been expecting the question. 'I think it would be unwise,' he said. "If we do go ahead, whether with one of these people or someone else, then I suggest we have one rule: no paper if we can help it, and if we can't, the minimum, kept in the hands of one person. Me.'

At last Sunnenden spoke. 'I'll need to think, but I guess I can remember all I need to know. You're right about keeping the paper down.'

He reached forward to switch on the ignition, changed his mind and settled back, still holding the sheets in his left hand.

Sunnenden stared straight ahead, thinking about his position, about the Secretary's fast-approaching visit to Moscow. He had not been invited along, even although Soviet affairs were his subject, and then there was Scott's fixation about this Zorin business ...

He turned his eyes back to the papers. He scanned one page of Cory's notes and absorbed a succession of facts: Russian speaking, physically okay for impersonating Zorin, a loner ...

Attached to it was the man's FBI tear sheet. Sunnenden held it out so that Cory could see what he was reading.

On the FBI sheet there was a line of request abbreviations, followed by five lines of the computer's acknowledgement. And then the detail: 'NCIC SUMMARY. MULTIPLE STATE FBI IT/23122X. (Date inquiry 11/25/75). EH. PARKER, JOHN C. MW ...'

It was the file over which Cory had worried so much.

Sunnenden stabbed it with his finger. '*This* looks like the man.'

Cory pointed to the bottom of the sheet. 'I agree,' he said. 'But there's one small problem.'

The line he indicated was headed 'Custody status.' It read: 'CAO699451D STATE PENITENTIARY FOLSOM CA 062068 RECEIVED.'

'As you see,' said Cory in his gentlest voice, 'he is still in prison.'

CHAPTER 7

Zorin averted his eyes as he left the courtyard, but even so he was conscious of one man leaving the car to follow him.

It had ceased to bother him. He was filled with a weariness; he felt burned out. But even so he tried to pull himself tall, to walk with a purposeful stride, for his shadow's benefit.

He was on his way to the bath house—one of the few habits he had continued to pursue after his release. Not to go would be too final a snub to old friends who gathered there and whom he now saw less and less.

The first week after his release had been surprisingly easy to endure despite his aching for Tanya. There had been a constant flow of solicitous friends, many lobbying and sending letters and telegrams, and there had been his own reaction : a mixture of numbness, of not quite accepting what had happened, coupled with anger and a desire to hit back.

After that it had grown bad. The friends still came, but a despair began to replace the numbness and anger. The attacks in the journals and the newspapers, the letters (orchestrated) praising the leadership for acting as they had over Tanya, and the way his neighbours turned their heads when he passed began to wear upon him as no previous harassment had.

The telephone became an instrument of torture. Local calls got through. International ones, whether from Tanya or friends in the West he did not know, were allowed through for just the brief second to let him know there was a call—and then cut off. At other times the telephone would ring and when he answered there was nothing but heavy breathing.

After his first flush of wanting to act, friends had persuaded him to keep quiet for a while, to lie low. 'There is nothing you can achieve at the moment,' they said. 'Keep quiet. Keep calm. Do not let them provoke you. What good will you be in Siberia?'

Soon there was no need for anyone to persuade him to do little. A helplessness took over. All he wanted to do was move through life without feeling. Nothingness by day, sleep by night, became his ideals, even if he did not achieve them. Small tasks became major efforts. He ate when he felt he had to, went out only when it was necessary. Friends who feared he might take his life checked drawers for tablets when he was not looking.

Suicide, though, was one possibility Zorin did not consider. His problem in fact was that there seemed no possibilities. There was a past but no future or rather a future he could not bear to contemplate. Inside he wanted to cry, to burst. Outside there was just a burnt-out face and a forced smile.

What had the KGB man said? 'You intellectuals love to suffer.' Perhaps it was true. Perhaps they had a capacity for it.

His friends saw his desperation for Tanya and sympathised and comforted as best they could, but their visits decreased as Zorin's mood became less and less sociable. What they could not sense was his fear. That again was a middle-of-the-night thing. The nightmares would come: of death creeping over him and he unable to move, or being buried alive and unable to speak to tell the gravediggers not to throw on the earth ... There were nightmares within nightmares. Was it really a dream? Was it happening again? He struggled to burst out through the layers of sleep away from the horrors, only to lie sweating and panting and wondering for many seconds whether he was really at home or in some ward.

It took him a half hour to reach the bath house. His KGB shadow followed him through the entrance door, but not further inside into the changing rooms. Zorin knew he would remain there—KGB men had an understandable reluctance to undress and be parted from their clothes and documents in a bath house where dissidents were known to gather.

There were only two other men in the steam room. Zorin nodded to them, but did not speak, even though he knew them both. Although he wanted to spend this token time with other dissidents he did not want to be drawn into discussions that might lead to him being asked to re-involve himself in their activities.

He settled on a slat in the least hot part of the room to acclimatise himself, closed his eyes, and wished the heat could ease his mind as well as his muscles.

The door opened and a newcomer entered. Zorin noted that the two men already there ceased talking. Moments later they left. Whatever they had been discussing they obviously did not want the newcomer, the poet Kukhlov, to hear. Zorin moved to a hotter part of the room, making way for Kukhlov. Although he still did not speak, he gave the poet a warm smile.

He knew why the other two had been suspicious: Kukhlov wrote the kind of poetry that the State liked. He came to the bath house because other poets gathered there, but no one discussed secrets in front of him. He just *might* be an informer.

Zorin, though, knew otherwise. He had read some of the poems Kukhlov had published abroad under another name, unknown to any but a close few. Zorin knew because the two men had sometimes secretly worked together.

'I've been here each day looking for you,' Kukhlov

said, moving closer. 'You must listen. There is a lot to say and someone may come in.'

Zorin instinctively looked towards the door.

'Tanya,' he said. 'You have news?'

'She is pregnant.'

'Pregnant?' Zorin's voice held disbelief. They wanted children, had tried often, but had become reconciled to childlessness even though, physically, they knew there was nothing wrong. 'It can't be.'

'I am told there is no doubt.'

Zorin began to remember Tanya's feelings of being slightly unwell just before they were arrested. He began to grin inanely, suddenly filled with a surge of joy.

Then he remembered. A child he would never see?

Kukhlov kept darting nervous glances towards the door.

'Please,' he said. 'I know how you must feel. But I must say the rest.'

'The rest? She's all right?'

'Yes, perfect. And the best attention. No, it is a question for you from friends in the West. They want to know if you would leave if the chance came. Leave without permission, without papers. Just leave secretly.'

Zorin made to speak.

'No. Think. Be sure. Take time.'

This time the grin was wider. It became a laugh. A child!

'Time to think?' he said. 'You must be mad, my friend.'

CHAPTER 8

Parker woke and without looking at his watch knew it was 5.30. Prison is a place of rigid and unchanging timetables. To those unchanging and rigid timetables enforced by Folsom prison, Parker had added his own. Now, like the 5.30 awakening, they had become a part of him, a kind of glue that helped him hold together.

He closed his eyes against the 25-watt bulb that burned above; if he had been allowed one wish in prison it would not have been for women or drink but for darkness when he wanted it. The only escape was to pull the blankets over your head—but if you fell asleep like that, you were liable to be wakened by a guard ripping off the covers to make sure it really was you and not a dummy.

He eased himself back on his pillow, placed his hands behind his head and began the quarter hour he allowed himself to savour the comparative quiet of the hour. Each morning at this time he let his mind go blank until images of places began to fill it. As soon as one emerged that pleased him he tried to hold it, examining it as one would a painting. Today it was a lake, viewed from halfway up a hillside. He recognised it immediately: a spot on the old Johnson ranch. From the vantage point, he could even re-call the occasion when his mind had photographed it. It was November, just a few days before Thanksgiving, and his father had stopped the car so that he could get out and admire the view. The image faded, and for the first time Parker checked his watch. It was 5.56.

He rolled out of his bed and remade it immediately. The cell was six feet wide, nine feet long, and a little over seven feet high. Apart from the bed, it had a locker, a sink with cold water, a stool, a commode, and two shelves filled with paperbacks.

Parker's other belongings were on the floor. Now he transferred them to the bed where they would remain until the night. There was a portable typewriter, bought with the money he received for his legal advice to prisoners. It stood on a plywood board which doubled as a chessboard. The chessmen, in a box on the shelf, were flat squares of wood each marked with the name of the piece. To type or to replay famous chess games he placed the board on the stool and sat on the edge of the bed. There were more paperbacks and a number of writing pads, each containing notes taken from law books obtained from the State Library on order. He often thought it ironic that, having renewed an interest in law to help himself, he had been forced to the conclusion that he was one man for whom the law held no hope. His work had, however, been a blessing. In prison you needed a hustle to survive well. One of the earliest pieces of advice he had been given was, 'It's surprising how must it costs to live in here.'

Parker had gone through the first eighteen months without a real hustle. That was when he had given up cigarettes so as not to run up debts to anyone. It had taken him that long to find one.

It was a good one, though. Parker's work was regular and well-paid. More important, as an inmate lawyer he enjoyed a position of great esteem. For the last five years Parker had not even carried a shiv. One major reason was that many tough men were beholden to him.

Even though he knew them by heart, Parker peered at the table of exercises on the wall. He was working his way through the Canadian 5BX and, after six years, he had reached—and exceeded—his limit.

He was wearing only shorts, and the cold of the concrete floor made him gasp when he came to his sit-ups. He did nineteen without pause.

The exercises finished, he washed with cold water from the sink, dried himself vigorously and then sat on the edge of the bed, the towel round his shoulders.

It could not be seen in the dim light but his face was almost grey, the special colour of men who see too little sun. But his body was in good shape. On one thing he went along with the Black Muslims who were always exercising in the yard: pride in your body does matter when you're inside. He reflected, as he often did at this moment of the day, that he looked like a different man from the one who had entered seven years before.

God, he had been flabby then. Before he had tightened up, before the lines had come, the pudginess had made him look even younger than he was at the time: twenty-eight. He recalled the moment he had changed. Three things had taken place within two days and afterwards he was never the same.

The first was that, through curiosity, he had found himself present at a homosexual 'wedding'. The 'bride' had been complete with dress and train and veil and had said 'I do' with a bashful lowering of eyes. Parker had been more fascinated than repelled. The second had been hearing the screams and later the cries of a homosexual gang bang. On entering prison, being raped had not been among Parker's many fears; after a few weeks it had become a constant one.

Whenever he looked back he thought perhaps he had willed the event that followed. Two men who had seen him at the 'wedding' had followed him to the showers. They were not hard to fight off, but it was obvious this was only the beginning. The following afternoon, the piece of pipe hidden inside his shirt, he approached them in the yard. While they were still grinning he landed blows on both. He kept hitting until the guards dragged him off. He could still close his eyes and see the blood and hear the whimpers from one, as he tried to shield his face with an arm that Parker promptly broke. And he could hear his own cries over and over again, 'I'm a man, you mother-fuckers. I'm not anybody's ass.' He was told later that he was lucky the two hadn't died, but from that moment he was established as a man to be left alone; from then on the prison ceased to dominate him.

At the far end of the tier Parker heard a stick being scraped across the bars. Again, without looking, he knew the time : 6.20. The noise grew louder as the convict turn-key approached. He was followed minutes later by another trusty with a large metal can of hot water. Parker watched as the spout was pushed through the bars and hot water poured into a bucket. Lifting it, Parker filled the sink and began to wash.

In a few minutes the guards would begin the morning count—the official start to a day just like over 2,500 others he had endured. How many thousands more, he wondered, still to face before he left this place—*if* he ever did...

Cory had first met Foster Williams when he was still with the police force, a young detective five years out of the Army, detailed to collate all the field reports on Robert Kennedy's assassination. Cory recruited him to inform the Company of *everything* that was emerging. At Cory's suggestion the Company later persuaded Williams, now a lieutenant, to go private. They supplied him with a fixed contract as security consultant for a company doing de-fence work; in addition, there had been the occasional special job—and this was his main worth.

He and Cory met at the Los Angeles Marriott Hotel. Cory began by explaining that the job was not for the Company but that authorisation for it came from the 'highest Washington levels'. Williams was to visit a prisoner in Folsom and sound him out about his willingness to do an unspecified task for a group in return for being got out. Cory supplied no details, but said it should be made clear to the prisoner that it was dangerous, would take him some weeks, and that he had every chance of surviving. In return the group would then give him money, false papers—a fresh start anywhere in the world he wished.

'You're to give no indication of who you're representing,' Cory told him. 'If he thinks you're the Mafia, so much the better.'

He then handed Williams a file and dozed in an armchair while the detective read it.

Williams finally looked up and said, 'I may need more of a lever than just his freedom.'

Cory, knowing the file by heart, sensed Williams' unspoken question. He reached into his breast pocket and took out a snapshot of a small girl. He handed it over. 'Give him this—but only it you have to,' he said. 'And tell him we can deliver her too.'

Parker collected his meat and rice and bread and placed himself among friends. He ate quickly. From now until the 3.20 count he was free to go to the library, walk in the yard, or return to his cell. Then he was scheduled to hold a law seminar in the yard, but the loudspeaker message ordered him to report to the assistant warden's office.

He walked there unhurriedly, feeling better with the warmth of the food in his stomach and the extra piece of bread in his pocket for later. His face showed no concern about the reason for the call—he was damned if he was going to show it. For one wild moment he wondered if he was to be moved or even paroled. But he knew that was not going to happen. Not to him. With luck they would think of releasing him when he had done twenty years.

The assistant warden was waiting, a single sheet of paper in his hand.

Parker stood in front of him, until gestured to sit down.

'You've a request for a visit,' said the assistant warden. Normally a guard would have put the request to the prisoner. But Parker was special. He had no approved list of visitors. Nor had he had a visitor in seven years.

'Who is it?'

'A man called Williams. He's a private investigator.'

Whatever it was about could do him no good other than satisfying his curiosity.

'Thank you. But I don't care to see him.'

The assistant warden nodded. He knew why the investigator wanted to see Parker; something to do with an unsolved robbery. He had also warned Sacramento that he doubted Parker would agree. Still he had better repeat what he had been asked to say. 'It's your right, Parker. But I think you ought to know it's something about your daughter.'

Parker desperately wanted to ask for reassurance: She's all right, isn't she? Say she's all right.

Instead he forced himself to grin. But the words seemed someone else's when he finally spoke.

'I'll see him, sir.'

Williams quickly noted Parker's physical points, but other features interested him more: the well-fitting prison garb, for example, gave some indication of his standing in the prison. Williams had the advantage of knowing Parker's background; he was very conscious of the fact that he knew very little about Parker's conduct over the previous seven years. This could be crucial.

Parker walked over and pulled back the chair. Williams allowed a few seconds to pass before looking at his watch, a reminder to the other that time was limited.

'So?' Parker said at last.

Williams leaned forward so that his face was nearer the mesh. The room was large enough for the guard not to be able to hear. Nevertheless Williams spoke so quietly that Parker was forced to strain himself to hear.

'It's only indirectly about your daughter. Friends have seen her—she didn't see them—and she is well.'

His tone became more conversational. 'I have friends who think it is a pity you're here and she is there, particularly as they know the truth. What they'd like to do, with your help, is remedy this situation.'

Forcing himself not to rush, he outlined the offer. He tried to place himself in the other's position. Parker's mind would be running through all the unspoken questions and possibilities: was this an elaborate frame-up? And if so, why? And why now? What enemies had he? Or, come to think of it, what friends?

'Why me?' said Parker.

'You've got some talent my friends would like to use. The rest you have to take on trust.'

Parker nodded his head slowly from side to side. 'No go.' His voice was firm. 'You could offer me freedom, an island in the Pacific and the Empire State building ...'

'We're offering you freedom and your daughter.'

Williams noted a barely perceptible response in the prisoner's eyes. He pressed on. 'All I can tell you is that my friends would want you to take a trip.'

'A dangerous trip?'

Williams' reply was indirect. 'The price they're paying is high.'

He was relieved when Parker let the conversation move on. 'Supposing I believed you, how would I know you were on the level?'

Williams smiled for the first time. 'You'd be out, wouldn't you?'

Parker allowed himself a smile too, and Williams hurried on. He could not hope for an answer now; Parker had to think on it.

'Just consider the proposition. That's all I ask.'

'And?'

'And if it's yes, all you have to do is *refuse* to see me again. In two days' time I'll put in a request for another visit. You tell the warden no. Then I'll know it's on. If you say yes, I'll know it's no go. Don't worry, I won't turn up whatever answer you give.'

He checked his watch. Five minutes left.

Parker was half smiling as though he took none of it seriously. 'And if I wanted to go ahead ...?'

'Then you wouldn't do anything. From then on matters would be taken care of by my friends.'

He waited until the door behind him opened, and a guard gave a two-minute warning. He smiled, took out the photograph, held it near the mesh. He felt Parker tighten. For a moment he was glad there was wire mesh between them.

'While you're thinking,' said Williams, 'remember this ...'

Parker did not even try to sleep. The photograph had reawakened parts of him that he had kept submerged for years.

There were two ways, he felt, to survive mentally in prison. The first was to live the important part of your life in day-dreaming; to pretend that it's the prison part that is a bad dream. Parker had done this for the first eighteen months of his sentence. The second way, which he had since adopted, was to face prison full on, to impose your personality upon it.

In practice it meant filling the day with events: exercising, reading, writing, working out chess moves. He accepted the fact that prison confined you, but you lived as fully as possible within those confines. Above all, you lived your sentence as it came day by day. You did not live in the future, nor, as so many did, in the past. This meant not clinging to what was lost, not reliving events, including mistakes. It also meant seizing satisfaction from what pleasures were available—an extra hunk of bread, a shot of good booze—and not dreaming of the freedom that would, or might, come one day.

For over five years he had fought not to think of it. It had become easier but never too easy. It was like being a drunk off the booze for a long time—Williams had uncorked the bottle and placed it in front of him.

Parker thought of the practical and immediate questions. Why should the offer be made? What did they want? Who were 'they'? And how—if he agreed—would he be sprung? He did not doubt Williams's seriousness; he knew when a man meant what he said. His mind debated the question of who Williams represented, but dismissed it as unanswerable. It could be anyone.

But why? His visitor had said 'to take a trip', and by his silence had conceded it was dangerous. What kind of trip? Why him? That was the most puzzling question. What qualification could he have that others had not? He shrugged. He knew there was only one way he would learn that. Whether he ever would . . .

It was not until well into the night that Parker allowed himself to remember.

He had been twenty-five when they met, a year out of the army, working with cars in the day and studying law at night. The couple who had raised him had just died, the wife first, the husband only weeks later.

Marion had filled a great void. She had moved in with him after the first week, treating him with an elaborate and protective kindness; she had even cried when he had admitted he couldn't remember his real parents, who were German.

He knew only that they had been killed in one of the Allied air raids. It was then that he had learned his Russian: a child begging from and working for the Russian occupiers of his part of Berlin. Memories were hazy and unreal now. It was strange to think how different his life might have been if he had not crossed into the American zone and been adopted by a childless American sergeant and his wife who changed his name from Reinhold to theirs, Parker.

Parker clenched his eyes, tried to reconstruct a real picture of Marion. He couldn't. He could remember blonde hair, a large bust that was at times motherly and at other times a dancing mouthful. But that was description; his mind refused to see or feel her.

Their first year was good. Gradually Parker slipped back on his schooling, but that gave him more time with Marion. The only problem was money; she liked to buy things and he wanted her to. Parker found himself doing small repair jobs in the garage and pocketing the money.

Finally he had been caught and advised to find another job. Because of that and partly because Marion was bored, Parker sold the house and furniture, spent some of the money on a new car, and they headed West.

In Reno they actually got married. Then they drifted for a few months, living on what was left of the house money until that was gone. Parker got another garage job in a small town in the Salinas Valley. The garage owner helped them find a home, a trailer in a small park on the edge of town.

Parker swung himself off the bed and felt the mattress until he found what he wanted: a bottle. He opened the seam and pulled it out. It was a pint of Jim Beam. He'd been saving it for a massive drink on his birthday, a day he always celebrated. He got back on the bed. Still fully dressed, he began drinking from the bottle.

Everything had seemed to go wrong from then on, even the nicest thing of all—that Marion was pregnant. Jonesville bored her; pregnancy was a ball and chain. She constantly goaded him with demands for more money, alternating these with threats to abort herself. The demands he tried to answer by working longer and longer hours; the threats by a mixture of warnings and pleadings. He wanted fatherhood in a way he had never wanted anything.

The baby was a girl. They called her Susan, and for a while Marion liked dressing the child and showing her around. The novelty wore off, but Parker was not sure that things wouldn't have been all right anyway if the two men had not arrived.

Marion said one was her brother from Miami, and the other his friend. They were waiting when he arrived home one evening. Both were well dressed, and the brother, Brad, carried a fat roll of money. At dinner Brad disregarded Parker, staring at his oil-encrusted hands and hinting that he had expected better things for his sister. Marion remained silent, not defending Parker . . .

He heard a noise at the end of the tier, and knew instinctively that it was a guard making an unscheduled round. He stoppered the bottle and rolled under the blanket, remaining still until the guard reached his cell and the flashlight roamed over him. He sat up, leaving the blanket where it was, and took another deep swallow of bourbon.

He wanted to believe that the reason he had accepted Brad's proposition was his fear that Marion might leave him, taking Susan with her. He could have borne losing a wife; his daughter was different. She was just over a year old, just beginning to take her first faltering steps, and he was already worrying about finding a house where she would have more room.

Brad's friend—in all that time Parker only knew him as Mac—left first. Brad and Parker followed two days later. Parker told his boss that there were family problems back home in Chicago and he would return in a week.

When Parker returned to Jonesville, it was not to work.

The raid went wrong from the start. The set-up was supposed to be that the day guards had been bribed to offer no resistance. Brad said there would be no violence. As soon as they stopped the van, the guards would come out, throwing down their weapons. The guns that Parker, Brad and Mac carried were only for show—to substantiate the guards' stories when they reported the hold-up. Brad claimed later that the crew had been changed, but Parker did not know the truth. The guards emerged shooting. Parker got hit in the leg, and one guard was badly hurt.

Parker was left in the road, and the other two were picked up within twenty-four hours. He drew a light sentence—as a result of favourable testimony from the police who were rewarding him for his co-operation, although that 'co-operation' was largely due to their refusal to take him to hospital until he talked.

At Florida State he had been allowed out on a work party almost from the start. On his third day on the party, other prisoners tried to escape. A guard had been bribed to shoot high. Parker went with them, more afraid to stay than to run.

He made his way back to Jonesville, desperate to know what was happening there. He waited until night to check the trailer. He tried the door and it opened.

They were there. He heard the sounds before he saw them.

The bedroom door was open. At first Parker thought the cries were the whimpers of an animal and then, halfway to the door, he realised he was hearing a woman making love.

He pushed open the door and there was a frozen moment before his eyes. He was surprised that the pain went as deep as ever. The bedroom was in semi-darkness. He could just make out the crib and the child's face, pushed against the bars, eyes wide. A yard away a single sheet covered the two moving bodies.

Then the scene exploded. Susan screamed. The man swung himself off the bed, reaching for something on the chair. The woman pulled herself up. Almost too late Parker realised the man was raising a gun. He moved in and, in his mind, the grappling was in slow motion.

There was a shot, not loud, more a plop, muffled by the stomach pressed against the barrel. The woman's scream joined that of the child. The man had fallen and was curled in the corner and Marion was tearing at Parker now. He pushed her away and realised, for the first time, that he held the gun. It was a .38 special, from the feel of it.

Parker clenched his teeth and felt the sweat beading on his forehead. He breathed deeply, willing himself not to be sick. At the trial, his counsel claimed everything that happened next happened during a few seconds of passion, but Parker knew otherwise. True, there was passion and hate and hurt. But everything he did in those seconds was calculated. The man was alive and moaning, curled, clutching his stomach. Marion was on the bed, her hands raised to protect her face. Parker shot her first, once in the chest and once in the head. Then he emptied the gun into the man. He dropped the gun on the floor, picked up Susan, carried her into the living room, and held her tight as he used the telephone.

When the police arrived they were gentle until the child was taken from his arms, and then, once they had seen that the dead man was their own police chief, one pistol whipped him until he lost consciousness.

Parker lifted the bottle high and poured until it overran the corners of his mouth. Then, staggering, he undressed, replaced the almost empty bottle and climbed into bed. It was nearly four.

He was now drunk enough to sleep.

'You should have pushed him,' said Cory.

Williams and Cory were holding another nighttime meeting, again at the Marriott. Cory had stayed on; there was nothing he could do back in Washington until he knew the answer.

Williams shrugged. He had done the right thing and Cory knew it. The older man was just suffering the nerves of impatience. Well, he would have to live with it.

He put down the sandwich.

'You're sure,' Cory said for the second time that night, 'that he understands that without us he'll just go on rotting?'

'I'm sure.' Williams picked up a turkey sandwich from a plate on the coffee table. The bread was curling in the heat. Williams took a bite. The meat was dry, too.

'He's been inside seven years,' said Cory. 'The time a lifer usually gets considered for parole.'

'Yes,' said Williams, 'but not with a dead cop on his record. Especially in a town like Jonesville.'

Cory wiped a hand across his forehead.

'I'm tired,' he said. 'You're calling the prison at what time?'

'Eleven. I'll let you know.'

Parker tried to evaluate the problem carefully and dispassionately. Throughout a sleepless night he continuously listed the arguments for and against co-operating.

On the balance side, he would be out of prison. Hopefully, too—although he could not be sure—whoever did it would have enough organisation to *keep* him outside.

Like most prisoners Parker had toyed with the thought of trying to escape. The problem of remaining free, without money, papers, or help, was one of the reasons Parker had never considered it seriously.

There was also the promise that he would be reunited with his daughter, although that was something that would have to be taken on trust. Even so, he ought to be able to exercise some sort of control over that—insist on guarantees before undertaking whatever job he had to do. Even see that money was deposited for her; that would be something...

On the debit side, there were many arguments: he had done seven years and one day he would be paroled—why risk it?

There was even a lingering fear of how well he would survive outside Folsom: he had licked life inside, but outside...

And how free would 'freedom' be: would he have to keep running? He wished he could ask them questions, even though he knew he would have to take the answers on trust.

But all the reservations and fears kept coming back to just one: *he didn't know what they wanted him to do*. It could, for all he knew, be an operation from which his chances of survival were small—or even nil.

In the early morning he exercised through habit, the same few questions and arguments running through his mind.

Would it matter if it was *that* dangerous? Wasn't almost anything preferable to the almost certain fact of spending another twenty years inside Folsom? He dismissed that: Folsom was better than death. Full point. But if he saw that Susan was taken care of...

He continued to wrestle with the problem through breakfast and afterwards, as he tried to work in the library.

When the summons came soon after eleven, he was still undecided.

This time the assistant warden was noticeably curious. 'You've another request for a visit?' he said, his expression questioning.

'The same man?' Parker knew the answer but had to be sure.

'Yes.'

Parker was quiet for so long that the deputy governor prompted him: 'Parker!'

There was still silence. The assistant warden made as though to speak again, but the prisoner's look stopped him: Parker was staring ahead, his eyes fixed as though on a vision.

Finally when he did speak his voice was sympathetic. 'Parker, your answer?'

And Parker, who was gazing at the face of a young girl, hardly recognised his own voice as he said, 'No, no, I won't see him.' After all the careful and dispassionate inward debate the decision was made—emotionally. Whatever the price he would pay it.

Williams had to awaken Cory to break the news even though it was 11.40 in the morning. Cory came to the door, stumbling, still half asleep.

'It's go, go, go, go,' said Williams the moment he was inside.

The decision was the prelude to two hectic days for Cory.

First he flew to Nassau, where he collected a message which told him to stay overnight in a certain hotel room. The next morning, again following instructions, he took a cab back to the airport where he was directed to a private Cessna. The aircraft landed him on Little Kingmead Island less than an hour later.

The short drive from the airstrip revealed miles of trees which the driver explained had been imported from Florida to fill the bare stretches of space. Cory noted a new golf course fringed by expensive holiday homes and, where the road touched the coast, work in progress to enlarge a natural harbour.

He congratulated Louie Rosen on the improvements when he reached the house, a white bungalow made distinctive by its high walls and guard dogs—to protect his art collection, as Louie always explained to new visitors.

Louie Rosen greeted Cory warmly. 'It's nice of you to say that. I'm kind of proud of it myself. A man needs something to occupy himself in his retirement and if he can do something like taking a beautiful place and making it more beautiful, well ...'

He insisted that Cory change and bathe before lunch, after which they sat on the porch and sipped cool drinks.

It was not until late in the evening that the two men talked business.

'I've retired,' said Cory. 'Just like you've retired.'

Louie acknowledged the tribute to his power with a faint smile.

Cory explained his request. Louie listened, curled in a huge black leather chair, looking like an elderly gnome.

At the end he asked one question.

'Why come to me, why not use people on the Coast?'

Cory replied, 'I know you, Louie. I don't know them.' Cory could have said 'You owe me.' It was not necessary, and he knew it.

Louie stood and offered cigars which Cory refused. He lit his own, taking exquisite care.

'Best Havana,' he said. 'Direct from Castro. Paying me back in cigars for the casinos he stole.' He laughed and returned to the subject of Cory's request. 'I'd need to ask the boys on the Coast.'

'Of course.'

A polite formality, they both knew.

Louie walked to the door and opened it. 'Get me Georgie,' he said to the man outside.

Georgie appeared seconds later. 'Yes, Mr Rosen.'

'Georgie,' said Louie, 'you're a lucky man. I'm sending you off to get some smog. There are some people I want you to take messages to.'

Five minutes later, Georgie dismissed, the two men shook hands.

'I appreciate it, I really do,' said Cory. 'You know that.'

'Don't, Jim,' said Louie. 'Don't thank me.' He stood back and opened his arms wide. 'What would life be if a man couldn't do a simple favour for a friend?'

CHAPTER 9

It had been almost a week since Parker had seen his visitor and five days since he reached his decision. The only result so far had been a hangover, noted and commented on by other inmates but not in front of Parker.

They were sure the visitor brought him bad news about his daughter.

Parker knew what they were thinking and let it go. It provided a reason for his transparent shock. The visitor's offer made him think of freedom as a serious possibility for the first time for years. Making the decision had been difficult: prison was bad but bearable, and the alternative was the unknown.

But once the decision was made, Parker expected it to be easy. And it was not. He smelt freedom and as the days passed by he began to sweat and panic that it had never been serious, or that something had gone wrong. Suddenly he faced endless more years inside, and he had lost his ability to cope.

Still he forced himself to follow his self-imposed routine: wake at 5.30, fifteen minutes of pleasant thoughts, exercise ... But the visit had its effect. Where he had always worked hard at the exercises, he now forced himself to limits as though the pains of exercising would cleanse him of his thoughts. He developed a habit of drifting off into fantasies he had always avoided—what *would* it be like? And he pictured himself with Susan.

The relief when something happened was so great that he began to shake as though he had a fever. The water had just arrived and he was shaving when the guard stopped outside the bars.

'After breakfast,' he said. 'Assistant warden wants to see you.'

This time the man had in front of him a whole file. He spoke slowly, savouring his own words, wanting to enjoy the other's reaction.

'The Adult Board has decided you should be revaluated,' he said. 'You realise what that means?'

Parker did. He had seen it happen to others. You went to Chino, the prison everyone entered when first convicted. You were put through a battery of tests. From those and from the many reports, recommendations were made to one of the boards. The result might be back to Folsom. It could also be transfer to a less stringent prison or, unlikely in Parker's case, parole.

He made himself smile. 'Thank you, sir.'

'Don't thank me. Lot to do before you can thank anyone.' He handed the file to one of the guards. 'But I think you have a good chance.'

Parker realised he was being dismissed. 'When do I go?' he asked.

The assistant warden looked surprised. 'Why, right now. This minute.'

There were two officers outside, waiting to escort him. Both were in civilian clothes. Before they signed for him, they had him stripped and searched. Then he was handed the clothes he had worn when he first entered Folsom seven years before.

They were so strange, so foreign that he could not remember them at first. When Parker tightened the belt of the brown trousers, they gathered round the waist. He must have lost four inches there. The jacket, on the other hand, would not button.

One guard noted Parker's struggles with the clothes with amusement. 'Don't sweat,' he said, 'you ain't going to no fancy parties.'

Once he was dressed they handcuffed his hands in front of him and chained his legs. 'Okay, let's go.'

Parker hobbled out of the door, along the corridor, across open ground and down into the tunnels. The car was parked just outside the walls, the engine already running. Parker was helped into the back, where his footchains were attached to a hook built into the floor. One guard got into the back with him, the other into the driving seat.

As the car drew off, Parker looked back at the prison. All he could take in was walls. He felt a strange mixture of emotions : elation at being out, and fear at being taken away from the familiar.

The guard in the back with him must have read his expression correctly. 'Don't you get worrying,' he said, 'we're probably gonna be bringing you right back to your little old cell before the month's out. No call to start getting homesick.'

Both guards laughed loudly. Parker joined them, realising that all three were sharing a collective need to release tension. Heading away from the prison brought release for the guards, too—even though they were men who walked out of the prison every day.

For most of the journey Parker sat still, drinking in the scenery. Open farmland gradually gave way to desert. The guards took turns driving and kept up a fast, even pace. They wanted to reach Chino in one day because they were allowed two for the journey. They could take a day free, perhaps spend it driving down to San Diego.

They ate at a drive-in restaurant and were back on their way in fifteen minutes. Parker fell asleep in the heat. When he awoke it was late afternoon. One of the guards offered him a can of beer and volunteered, 'We're just out of Mojave.'

Parker took the can and peeled back the tab. He drank, the warm beer trickling out over his chin.

'Better tell him,' said the guard up front to his colleague.

Parker drank again and waited. 'In a few minutes,' explained the guard beside Parker, 'we're gonna make a short stop. Just a coupla seconds. We hand something over, someone hands something to us.'

'So?'

'So you don't see nothing. Okay?'

Parker shrugged his shoulders.

'Good.' Both guards were smiling. 'There'll be a little something in it for you.'

Parker was not surprised. Prison walls could not stop the fact that some men wanted things and did not have them and others were eager to supply them. Over the years he found that it was easy to get almost anything in or out, provided you had the funds.

He dropped the empty can on to the floor and lay back, his eyes closed. 'I think I'll take another sleep,' he said.

He remained slumped, his eyes closed; the car began to slow and Parker felt it turn off the road and stop.

There was the noise of a window being wound down, and of footsteps approaching. He heard the sound of paper and the feet retreating, and then the car pulled back on to the road.

He heard the rustle of money; the guard beside him would be counting. 'All there?' asked the voice from up-front.

'Yes.'

'Good,' said the other guard. 'Hey, did you catch the guy in the car, the other one? He was using a two-way radio or something, I swear.'

'Reporting it had gone according to plan, I guess. Christ, these guys are organised.'

Parker waited a few more minutes and then opened his eyes and gave a loud theatrical yawn. 'Sure needed that sleep,' he said. 'Can't remember even dropping off.'

The guard next to him laughed and pushed a note into Parker's shirt pocket. 'Here,' he said, 'you dropped that while you were asleep.'

Parker thanked him, but did not look to see what denomination the note was. That would have been bad manners.

The guard checked his watch and then turned to look out of the window.

'Christ, it's deadman's country.'

The car rounded a bend, into the sun, and for a moment the driver was blinded. He pulled down the visor. 'Hey,' called the guard in the back, 'ease up, there's something up ahead.'

The car began to slow. Parker craned his neck to look ahead. 'Looks like some truck's turned over.'

The driver brought the car to a halt, but remained in his seat. The truck was on its side, its cargo of boxes scattered across the road. A car had pulled up a few yards away and a man, probably its driver, was kneeling beside what looked like a body.

Hearing the prison car, he stood up and hurried over. 'Hey,' he began shouting when he was a few yards away, 'you guys got a first-aid kit?'

The guard wound down the window. The man was close now. Suddenly his hand was at the window, and in it was a gun.

'Just open the door slowly,' he said, 'and don't do a damn thing.'

The door was opened and the man leaned in and removed the ignition key. 'Okay, now open the passenger door.'

He was a big man, well over six feet tall and built like a wrestler. His hair was cropped short and Parker noted that his eyes were narrowed like someone waiting for something to happen and showing he was ready for it.

The guard obeyed.

Beyond the man, Parker could see the 'body' lifting itself from the ground and getting into the parked car.

The man with a gun edged round the car, holding the weapon with both hands, pointed all the time at the guard in front.

He reached the passenger side and climbed in.

'Okay,' he said, handing back the ignition keys, 'we're doing fine so far. Now just pull past that truck and make the first right. It's a track, maybe two miles ahead.' He jabbed the gun into the other's side. 'Let's go.'

In the mirror, Parker saw the other car move off behind them.

'There.' The gunman was gesturing to a turn which could barely be seen. The track was pitted and seemingly unused for years. Parker reckoned they had been driving for about two miles since leaving the road when the gunman said, 'Okay, we stop now.'

The other car stopped. The gunman waited until its driver was outside before he ordered the two guards out. One of them turned to Parker who was still manacled to the floor.

'What about him?'

'Leave him where he is.'

The man from the other car carried two guns, a shotgun and a submachine gun. He tossed one to the man who had hijacked the prison car.

Parker thought at first that this was the move to free him, but now that he was left chained into the car, he began to feel real terror. He asked himself how they had known just *when* to block the road. He answered himself immediately. The handover minutes before! The men had been radioing ahead to set this in motion. That way they could ensure they got the right car.

'Now.' The man with the submachine gun was gesturing toward the desert. 'You two walk that way, keep walking and don't turn, whatever happens.'

The second man came towards Parker; his chains were unlocked and he was pulled, blinking and stiff, into the harsh sun.

The man said nothing, but went over to his own car, opened the trunk, and dragged out a sack. With effort, the two men dragged it to the prison car, both still clutching their guns.

They eased it into the back seat. The one with the submachine gun stepped back. The second man leaned into the car and looked as though he was opening the sack. Then he leaned back, his shotgun pressed inside, his body shielded by the door.

There were two shots. The first gunman noted Parker's shocked puzzlement.

'Teeth,' he said conversationally. 'Nasty things to leave intact. Too easy to identify.'

The second gunman moved away from the car and the one who had spoken to Parker raked it with submachine gun fire.

'They're not looking back,' said the other. Parker had forgotten the guards.

'Good, but better get him inside.'

Parker was led to the gunmen's car and put in the front passenger seat. One man sat behind him. The other was pouring gasoline over the prison car. Finally satisfied, he tossed in a burning clip of matches and jumped back. The car exploded into flames. The man was back in the car now, yelling 'Let's go.'

They reached the main road within minutes, screeched to a stop. The door was opened from inside and Parker was pushed out. Another car was waiting, a man leaning against it. He opened the door for Parker to get in.

'My friends say welcome,' said Foster Williams.

CHAPTER 10

Foster Williams drove at a fast steady pace for fifty minutes, and then stopped. Without speaking, he reached into the back of the car and produced two sets of flying coveralls.

Pulling on one, he gestured to Parker to do the same. Despite the confines of the car, it took only moments.

Williams reached round again and this time came up with two helmets with visors. He placed one on the floor near his feet, and gave the other to Parker.

'Keep this on your knee till I tell you,' he said. 'In about ten minutes you'll see an airfield. We're going flying.'

The getaway by air had been Cory's idea after a great deal of consideration. He wanted the guards to hear and see enough of what was happening to be convinced that the badly burned body found in the car was Parker's, Making them walk into the desert seemed the best way, but it meant they would be able to give the alarm in about two hours.

Louie had suggested transferring him to a compartment in a large truck. But the truck might be stopped, it might be searched. Whatever the cost, there must be no chance of Parker being discovered alive at this stage. For that reason, with reluctance, Cory sought official help.

The airfield—Edwards Air Base—came into sight almost exactly at the time Williams had calculated. The two men pulled on their helmets; behind visors they were unrecognisable.

At the gate, Williams' pass produced immediate entry

and directions to a helicopter pad where a pilot was waiting. He was not surprised that one man, the thinner one, said nothing on the whole of the five hundred mile flight to Phoenix: there had been enough hints for him to guess that the man was a defector the CIA had got out through Mexico and was now probably on his way to a 'safe house' in Arizona.

At Phoenix Williams produced a change of clothes and from there he and Parker flew on commercial flights; first to Chicago and then, using different names, to Pittsburgh before driving the last six hours of the journey to Washington.

This had presented Cory with his second major worry: where to hide and brief Parker for the next few weeks while he was being prepared for his mission. He wanted Parker to remain unsure of who was directing the operation. That meant somewhere other than Washington—ideally, a private house in an isolated location. Yet Washington was where the materials and people Cory needed were based. Conceding the reality that for the first two weeks at least he needed a place with all necessary facilities, he chose Camp Peary.

Again—reluctantly—he sought official help. He explained his needs to Sunnenden and within a day obtained what he wanted: an operation authorisation from the National Security Council, answerable only to the Secretary, allowing the use of the highest security classification. The operation itself was left vague.

From now on, Cory knew, natural secrecy would take over: the more he demanded, the less people would want to know.

Camp Peary stands in southern Virginia, a fifteen-mile drive from Williamsburg. The base was once a wildlife refuge, and its woods are still thick with deer. Today it is ostensibly a Defense Department research and testing station, hence the military police guards and barbed wire topped fences and signs saying 'US Government Reservation. No Trespassing.'

In actuality it is one of the most secret and closely guarded areas in the Western world. Much of its space is devoted to training new CIA men. Other areas of the camp are even more secret: on them special operations are planned, foreign agents briefed, defectors interrogated.

To gain illegal entry to the base at all—with its guards, electrified fences, dogs and tripwires—would be difficult at best; to enter one of the high security sections without authorisation would be almost impossible. It was in one of those areas that Cory chose his house.

Cory was waiting at the gatehouse when Williams' car appeared. It was nighttime. For the last twenty miles Parker had been lying on the floor, covered with a blanket —a small precaution but the best they could manage. Over the weeks they would add a number of others, along with pieces of false information, all meant to prevent Parker being totally certain for whom he was working.

Cory, standing inside the gatehouse drinking coffee, saw the car stop under the lights. He recognised the number before the guard shone a light on to Williams' face.

'That's him,' said Cory, putting down his cup. He went outside, opened the rear door.

'Don't sit up,' he said, lifting a corner of the blanket. 'I just want to see your face.' He stared for a long time. The face was more drawn than the photographs, but it was unmistakably Parker.

Cory stepped back. 'I'll take over from here,' he told the guard.

He climbed into the front seat next to Williams. 'Straight on, until the road forks,' he said. 'Then make a right. I'll direct you from there.'

He waved to the guard, who was on his way back into the gatehouse to phone the first check point. There were three. At each one Cory's face and papers were sufficient to get them through. No one asked to look under the blanket.

In the woods were other men, equipped with nightglasses, monitoring the car's journey and making sure, despite Cory's security clearance and rating, that it did not stop nor deviate from the designated route.

'In fifty yards, there's a track on the right,' Cory said at last. 'I'd slow now.'

'I see it.'

Williams turned off the narrow road. The track wound through trees; the car had to stop once to avoid deer. The house was in a clearing, its grounds lit by spotlights. There were no guards in sight; they had orders not to come within 250 yards unless called.

Williams and Cory helped Parker from the back seat, keeping the blanket over his head until they were inside the bungalow. It was comfortable but rudimentary inside —the kind of place someone might build as a holiday home. The walls and ceilings were wood panelled, the floor was cork blocks and the furniture and pictures—all of American scenes—had obviously come from the same stockpile. The only sign of individuality was in the main room: stacks of well-read paperbacks left by a succession of former occupants and their guards.

Cory dumped some parcels, then rummaged in one bag and took out a quart of Chivas Regal. He fetched glasses and poured three drinks.

'To your freedom,' he said and took a deep swallow.

Williams drank immediately, but Parker raised his glass slowly, looking hard at Cory. He sipped and let the neat liquor swish around his mouth. He took a second sip. Then at last he smiled.

'To my freedom.'

Parker finished the drink. Cory poured him another, and Parker took one sip. They were all still standing. Parker wiped his forehead. 'Christ, I'm tired.'

Cory stoppered the bottle and handed it to Parker. 'Drink it in bed,' he urged. When there was no response, he said 'I mean it.'

Parker took the bottle. Cory led him along a passage and into a small bedroom.

'We'll talk tomorrow,' he said, closing the door.

Parker noted that there was no handle on the inside. Somehow, it didn't seem to matter.

Parker woke, and without looking at his watch knew it was 5.30.

Then he did look, and it was almost nine.

He lifted himself up and looked over the edge of the bed to the floor. The near-ful bottle of whisky, carefully stoppered, was still there. He had finished his glass but poured no more: he had felt exhausted enough after the two days to be vulnerable without getting drunk. Moreover—and rightly—he suspected that the bottle was an initial test.

He spent a few minutes taking in the room, and enjoying the unfamiliarity of it—the couch, panelled wall, curtained alcove containing a shower. There were recessed spotlights in the ceiling and a standard lamp in the corner near the window. Looking at them, he realised another reason why he had slept so well: the darkness.

He saw that the door had been opened and left ajar, but he disregarded it and walked across to the shower.

Dried and dressed, he looked out of the window. There were birds on the grass. Despite the hour there was little sun: the trees were close enough to mask it until midmorning.

When he finally made his way to the main room, only Cory was there. He was standing in the kitchen filling a mug with coffee. He held it out towards Parker.

'Good morning,' he said, as though Parker's presence was the most natural thing in the world.

Parker took the mug, staring deep into Cory's face. He was wary, frightened almost. The escape and his hide-out showed that whoever had freed him was both highly organised and totally ruthless.

He tried to hide his anxiety. At least they wanted him alive. Clutching his mug, he started to walk to the window. Cory sensed his hesitation; it pleased him.

'Yes,' he said, 'you can go outside, but don't move away from the house. And I mean that. Never.'

Parker stood in the doorway, breathing in the morning air mixed with the smell of fresh coffee, enjoying the sounds of the woods. Behind him Cory began scrambling eggs in a pan.

They breakfasted together at the small scrubbed table next to the bar. Both men ate slowly and carefully, Cory because it was his habit, Parker because he did not want to be sick. He had suffered once already after eating onion soup and filet mignon and pie and ice-cream on the journey from California.

At last, the eggs and bacon finished, Cory fetched more coffee and spoke for the first time.

'You're a quiet man, Mr Parker, and I appreciate that. I'm a quiet man myself.' Cory lifted his mug and drank, his eyes wide above the rim, watching carefully. 'I also realise that the fact you are a quiet man doesn't mean you're not a curious one, but if I read you right you have managed to control that.'

There was sound of the front door opening and closing; Parker kept his attention on Cory.

'I'm afraid you'll have to continue to control it for a little longer,' Cory continued. 'I think that today you should rest. When we've finished coffee I'll show you around the rest of the house. Sleep or read or watch television, whatever you like. If you're hungry, eat.' He waved towards the living room where Parker could see bottles lined up on a shelf. 'If you're thirsty, drink. Tomorrow we'll start work.'

The door opened and Williams entered. Cory put down his cup. 'For now,' he said, 'I'll leave you.' To Williams he added, 'I'll see you tonight.'

He closed the door behind him and started along the passageway. A door opened quietly and Sunnenden stepped out to join him. For the past few minutes he had been watching Parker through the closed circuit television system.

Cory waited until they were outside.

'Happy?'

'God,' exclaimed Sunnenden, 'I think it's going to work.'

Cory closed the blinds while Williams set up the screen and projector. Parker, seated alone on the couch, watched the screen impassively.

The first scene was the outside of a building; Parker could not place its location. A man came into view and walked down a short flight of steps. He wore a jacket, an open shirt, a beret, and drew at a cigarette as he walked— as though for every mouthful of air he took he needed another of tobacco smoke. He was bearded, and he kept looking from side to side.

As he came closer, the picture became blurred and the film went blank. Another shot of the same man followed, this time standing with other people at what looked like an open-air party. In turn that image gave way to others: footage shot at a café, in a park, at a conference. Often the quality was poor: the scene was obstructed by moving bodies, or ruined by poor lighting. The one thing common to every scene was the bearded man.

The film lasted perhaps half an hour. At the end of it Cory clicked on the light.

'There are more,' he said. 'All I want you to do for now is keep watching them. I want you to *know* that man.'

Cory was rarely in the house during the next three days. For hours each day Parker watched films, mainly of the bearded man, but also ones showing the insides of buildings and other recurring faces. In the evenings he worked through portfolios of photographs. By the fourth day he could close his eyes and describe the things he had seen to the smallest detail.

His attempts to get any feedback from Williams had failed. His brief talks to Cory were confined to pleasantries.

Occasionally he heard cars arrive and depart; doors open and close. He sensed he was being watched, and suspected closed circuit television.

After a few days the combination of a taste of freedom without real freedom and the uncertainty of the immediate future began to get to him. He would wake earlier and stand by the window, watching the dawn and wondering about his chances of getting free.

With the lights out he was sure that he could not be seen on television, even if anyone was up to watch him. He was wrong on both points. On the screen the infrared light that bathed the room made it as clear as in daylight. Each night and early morning Cory sat by the screen, watching and calculating and planning.

On the sixth day the monotony of the routine was broken. Parker had just finished watching a film, for the tenth time. As Williams got up to change the film, Parker heard a car arrive at the front of the house. Then the door. It was Cory; behind him was another man, large, and baldheaded except for a few strands of hair carefully combed across from one side to another.

At their arrival, Williams left the room. The stranger beckoned Parker to stand under one of the lights, then opened the blinds and stood him by the window. He walked around him, as though studying a painting. He looked at Parker's skin and hands, patted his stomach, asked him to walk and to sit down and stand. Finally he took clips of Parker's hair.

During the whole of the examination nothing, apart from the stranger's one-word instructions, was said. Cory stood by the door, arms folded in front.

'Enough?' he asked when the sample of hair had been taken.

The stranger's tone was almost petulant. 'I'd still like to take pictures.'

Cory opened the door for him. 'You'll manage without. You know my feelings.'

Williams was waiting outside the door to lead the other away.

'You'll drive him to the airport?' asked Cory. Williams nodded.

Parker heard the front door close behind the two men. Cory smiled at him, a long smile, checked his watch and announced 'Cocktail hour', though it was only a little after midday. As on the first night, he poured two Chivas Regals, this time on the rocks.

'I imagine that you're getting a bit bored with the films by now,' he said. 'But life should get a little more interesting from now on. Apart from anything else, soon we'll move out of here—give you a new view.'

'I think it's time you told me what my freedom is going to cost me,' said Parker.

Cory raised his glass in a toasting gesture. 'You're right.' He gestured to the film projector that stood on a side table. 'The man in the film, did you recognise him?' Parker had not.

'Nor the place?'

That he had recognised, in some shots at least, 'Russia,' he replied.

Cory nodded. 'Good. Now what we want you to do is to make yourself look like the man in the film. And walk like him and stand like him. You've got a month. You'll get all the help we can give you, but you'll have to work.'

Cory held a packet of cigarettes out towards Parker. 'You'd better start with these. He smokes heavily.'

Parker took one of the cigarettes. It was greyish and had a crude filter. He accepted a light and smoked cautiously, not inhaling but holding the smoke for a few seconds before blowing it out.

Cory smiled. 'You can always give it up again.'

Parker altered his hold on the cigarette so that it was gripped between the tips of his fingers, much further from the filter than most smokers hold a cigarette. 'Good,' said Cory. Parker had absorbed the film well.

'Who is he?' asked Parker at last.

'It's of no consequence,' Cory said. 'That can wait until later.'

Parker tried a tentative inhaling of the cigarette and felt giddy. He stubbed it out.

'What happens when I do manage to look like him?'

Cory clinked the ice in his drink. 'Don't worry.' He anticipated a fear Parker would feel now or later. 'You're not going to wind up on a slab with people thinking you're him.' He smiled. 'We've done that one already.'

Cory reached in his pocket for his wallet and very carefully extracted a newspaper clipping. '*Los Angeles Times*,' he explained as he handed it over.

Parker read it slowly, his face impassive. It was an account of his own death. He wondered what his sister would think of it. The prison would have notified her anyway. Would she tell Susan her father was dead? He doubted it. They had agreed while he was awaiting trial, that Susan should simply be told her father had 'gone away'. He thought it unlikely his sister would change the story now.

He handed it back. 'It's an odd feeling, being a dead man.'

'You'll find later that it has advantages. No one looks

for a man who doesn't exist any more.'

'So what does happen when I look like him?' Parker repeated.

'Then,' said Cory, 'we send you to Russia to meet him. And you carry out a simple task. And then you come back and we settle you somewhere nice where no one knows you and you live happily ever after.'

'What if I don't come back?'

'We would be very unhappy,' said Cory.

CHAPTER 11

Before the end of the month, Cory moved Parker into a
large house in suburban Maryland. It belonged to a Pen-
tagon official, temporarily overseas. Although less secure
than Camp Peary, the house and grounds had advantages
over that site. Parker now needed frequent visits from
the makeup man and from the retired acting coach Cory
had found for him. There were as well the constant com-
ings and goings of Williams and Cory. Camp Peary was
not geared to such movement: in highly restricted sections men moved in, stayed for a long time and then left.
Cory was afraid he was stirring too many ripples.

In addition, he wanted Parker to start functioning
again in the outside world. At an outside house he could
at least say 'good morning' to neighbours, accompany
Williams or Cory to shops, be taken to movies and restaur-
ants. Parker still carried the look of a man who had been
institutionalised for a long time.

Besides, Cory now felt happier about Parker. He sensed
that the man had considered escape but had been sensible
enough to realise that without money, without documents,
without on identity he would not survive. Parker looked
a little less like a jail bird now: his hair had grown, so
had a moustache.

As far as the rest of the world was concerned Parker was
dead. The body had been accepted as his, and it had been
a simple matter for Denton to programme the national
and California State computers to destroy all references
to Parker. The only dossier that remained was his file in
Sacramento. Even this would go: at Denton's request

the local FBI would be asked to collect it. 'No one will question that,' Denton had explained, 'as long as they get a signature.' Back in Washington, it would vanish.

Cory told Parker he had a month, but he reckoned they still needed that much time once they moved into the new house. Like the headmaster of a school, he began to draw up work schedules.

Parker's days rapidly took on a pattern. They began with a short session under the sunlamp, to take away the prison grey, and then a fattening breakfast to bring him up to Zorin's weight. At first he resented this—it had taken years to get his body into such good shape, but then it became a kind of contest—how quickly could he do what was needed?

In the second week his training to impersonate Zorin entered a new phase.

The retired acting coach, found by Al, the makeup man, arrived with Williams just after ten. He still clutched his suitcase; the Los Angeles flight had been late and Williams had decided not to stop off at the man's hotel but to deliver him there later.

Parker watched him walk from the car from an up-stairs window: his training room. The man was small, thin, very pale and dressed in black, and reminded Parker more of a mortician than an acting coach.

Although he heard the front door open and close Parker did not go down. Cory, he knew, would want to talk to the man first.

Because of the newcomer, there was no session with the makeup man today, and Parker stretched on the couch, enjoying the inactivity.

When they had moved into the house, this room had been a bedroom. The bed, and a dressing table had been moved to another room and replaced with chairs.

The built-in closet and the chests of drawers no longer

held clothes but material needed in Parker's training: slide machines and projectors, files, and photographs.

One wall was covered with pictures and drawings of Zorin, his apartment and of Moscow.

Although Parker was not working, the room was filled with background sounds from the tape recorder: people speaking in Russian, part of Parker's 'refresher' course.

Gory turned it off when he entered the room with the acting teacher. He introduced the two men formally. 'Mr Hawkes, Mr Parker.'

The coach's hand was long and feminine looking, but surprisingly firm when the two shook hands.

'Mr Hawkes knows all about our problems, and he's going to help,' Cory began.

Hawkes acknowledged the introduction with a nod and immediately asked a question. 'Do you know *anything* about acting?'

Parker shook his head.

'Good.' He turned to Cory. 'Do you want to sit in on this?' It was obvious from his tone that he preferred to be alone with Parker.

Cory stood. 'I'll check that everything's set up.'

Hawkes waited until he had left. 'What you are going to do,' he said, 'is both harder and easier than acting on the stage.'

He began pacing the floor, gesturing with his hands as he talked. 'An actor,' he continued, 'can adapt a part to suit his own character and personality. He can decide to some degree what the person he plays should be like. You follow me?'

Parker was not sure, but he nodded assent.

'You, on the other hand, have got to play a specific man—just the way he is.'

'I know.'

Hawkes continued as though nothing had been said. 'It's been done. You remember Montgomery's double?'

Parker did. A soldier called James had been used by British intelligence during World War II to impersonate the British army leader in order to delude the Germans.

'Yes,' said Hawkes, as though thinking aloud, 'you've got some advantages—I gather you're to be seen mostly while moving in the street. Right?'

'So I gather.'

'And we don't worry about the voice?'

Again Parker agreed.

'Okay.' Hawkes looked at his watch. 'You know all about this man? You've studied him, seen moving pictures?'

'Yes. A lot.'

'Good. Let's try an experiment. I could give you a lecture on what you need to worry about, and maybe later I will. But first I want you to really *see* things . . .'

He walked towards the door. He turned as though surprised that Parker was not following him. 'Okay,' he said, 'grab your coat. Let's go.'

Williams drove the two of them about two miles to another quiet residential street. Neither he nor Hawkes said anything until they parked.

'Now,' said Hawkes, 'what I want you to do is simple. Just get out of the car and walk around until we pick you up again. Just go anywhere, do anything you want.' He paused and Parker waited, hand on the door handle, knowing there was more.

'Only one thing. You walk and act and behave as your man would. Okay?'

Parker walked aimlessly for almost a half hour before Williams picked him up again. During the time he did as Hawkes had requested, trying to remember and imitate the Russian's actions, but he found the exercise puzzling. Throughout there was no sign of Williams' car, though three times he spotted an identical van and was suspicious until he realised it was making local grocery deliveries.

His curiosity was not answered until two hours after arriving back at the house. Hawkes, Cory and Williams entered the training room with a small suitcase.

The room was darkened and Parker found himself watching a film of his walk. 'The delivery van!' he muttered aloud.

'Through the back window,' Williams agreed.

There were three snatches of film, the longest lasting eight minutes.

Hawkes said nothing until the end. 'Now let's watch it again,' he said. This time he made comments.

'Now note this carefully.' On the screen Parker was standing at the kerb waiting to cross the road. 'Standing, not moving. That's the hardest thing of all ...

'Okay, now watch that move there.' Parker was turning his head to look back. 'You're acting it up.'

The film finished.

Hawkes switched on the light. 'Give me ten minutes,' he said to Williams and Cory.

As soon as the two were alone, Hawkes gestured towards the empty screen. 'I wanted you to see that not because I want you to think you're piss awful, but because I want you to know what we've got to do.'

Parker remained silent. He was feeling abashed, nervous and angry at being made to look ridiculous in front of Cory and Williams.

Hawkes wiped his forehead with the back of his hand. 'I'll save the lectures for tomorrow,' he said. 'But I needed to show you that at present you're trying to act out the things you've seen your man do on the screen. Well, that's okay and you'll be doing lots of that. But you know what you have to do first?'

Parker shook his head.

Hawkes picked up one of the many pictures of Zorin that lay around the room. 'You've got to know *why* he does things. *Why* he stoops like that. *Why* he runs in a funny way, bent to the left. *Why* he chainsmokes. You tell me you *know* him. Okay, all you have to do now is *be* him.'

While lessons filled Parker's days and, often, some of the night, Cory was facing a further problem: establishing an identity for the man Parker would purport to be on his way into Russia.

On this Cory knew he could not work alone. He reserved a room at the Hospitality House Motor Inn and arranged a meeting there with a man from the Company's Technical Service Division. Neither man knew the other's name. Cory explained what he wanted: a background to fit a man between thirty-seven and forty-three, holder of an American passport, but preferably living abroad for some years. 'Then,' said Cory, 'I'll need all the bits of paper to go with it.'

'I'll need to check,' said the man. Cory was not sure whether he meant he would have to check the availability of such material or Cory's authorisation to receive it. He contented himself with saying 'Fine' and making a note to call Sunnenden. The two men arranged to meet again.

Despite all the arrangements to be made he tried to see Parker for at least two hours every day. Over the days he became increasingly impressed by him.

In the last week in April Cory slipped into the training room to watch the last minutes of an acting session. Hawkes glanced briefly towards him and then continued; he had ceased objecting to Cory's presence provided he did not interfere.

They were working on Zorin's walk. 'So tell me,' said Hawkes, 'why we get that walk.' He gestured towards the empty screen on which they had been watching film of the Russian before Cory's arrival.

'Stooping over a desk and work benches,' replied Parker.

'Good. That's the rounded shoulders and the head forward. Why then that stride?'

'Stubborn. Determined.'

'Good. What else?'

'Shuts off, mind wanders while he's walking.'

'And so?'

'So unless he's interested in something he only half sees. You can see that in the crowd shots.'

The doorbell rang. Cory checked his watch. It would be Al.

Hawkes nodded to Parker. 'Okay,' he said, 'go answer the door.'

'Like Zorin.'

Hawkes nodded.

At the door Parker paused and looked back. His face was tightened; he pulled his body taut; he was in command.

Hawkes waited until Parker was on the staircase and out of sight. 'He'll make it,' he said to Cory.

The following day Al arrived just as Hawkes was leaving. They nodded to each other. Although the two men had known each other many years, Cory and Parker had never heard them exchange more than a brief greeting.

Al set down his battered briefcase on the sofa and announced to Parker. 'Goodies for you today.'

Cory, who was again sitting in, noted Parker's strained face. 'You want a break?' he asked, concerned.

Parker focused on him. 'What? Oh no, I'm okay. It's just hard switching off.' He turned his attention to Al who was opening his case.

It was three days since Parker had seen him; the makeup man had been away working on some of the items he needed.

Al handed Parker a pair of spectacles with heavy frames. Parker put them on and walked over to a mirror.

He was surprised at how much they changed his face.

'Plain glass because of the contact lenses,' explained Al. And then, remembering, asked 'What about the contacts. Still all right?'

Parker had been wearing them a little longer each day. 'Up to six hours yesterday.' Al looked pleased. 'You've earned a bonus prize,' he said.

Even when the next object was handed to him Parker failed to see its purpose. 'It's a shoe heel,' he said at last. He turned it over. 'But with four studs on the top.'

'Good,' exclaimed Al, taking it back. He was beaming. In his spare time he did conjuring tricks for neighbours' children's parties. Sessions like this gave him similar satisfaction.

He removed one of his own shoes and pointed at the heel on it. 'It's pretty hard to limp,' he said. 'Believe me. You feign a limp and sure as hell you're gonna have to hurry to miss a car as you cross the street. And then, wham. You forget everything except moving your ass. And your limp's all gone.'

He placed the false heel against the real one. 'Now make four little holes in this heel,' he explained tapping the real one. 'Then slip in the studs on the other . . .'

He held the two together. 'There you are—one heel a half inch higher than the other foot. And, I tell you, you'll limp.'

'How easy is it to fix in operation?' asked Cory.

'Seconds. You could do it right in the street without taking your shoe off.'

'And to get rid of the limp?'

'Just slip it off and slide it into your pocket.'

'Nice,' smiled Cory. 'Nice.'

Al beamed. Cory's praise was like the clapping when the kids applauded his tricks.

'And now,' Al said, walking back to his bag and inserting a hand, 'the *pièce de résistance*.'

He held out the beard at arm's length until Parker took it.

Parker took off the spectacles before walking over to the wall mirror. Only then did he press the false beard into place. He smoothed the edges of his real moustache over the joins.

He stared for a long time before turning to face Cory and Al. Al began to speak, but Parker's eyes stilled him. Suddenly the room was very quiet.

Without knowing anything about the scheme to free Zorin, the Russian Colonel who left his Moscow office just before lunch was about to trigger the plot.

He headed away from the GRU, military intelligence, building and towards Gorky Park.

After a week of unseasonal showers the weather was dry and warm and there were crowds strolling and children playing inside the park.

The Colonel walked down the park's main central lane and then took a seat on a bench. Fumbling in his pocket, he finally found what he sought—a bag of sweets. He sucked one, enjoying the activity around him.

After five minutes he continued walking. A few yards away two children, aged about four and five, were playing. Their mother watched from a bench. The Colonel helped himself to another sweet and then, as if on impulse, he stopped by the children. He held out the bag. Both looked at the bag shyly and towards their mother for confirmation. She nodded. The children took sweets. 'And one for your mother,' said the Colonel. They looked as though they did not understand. He pointed. One, a girl, smiled. She took the extra sweet and ran to give it to her mother. The Colonel walked on feeling good.

He took another sweet, double-checking that the right ones had been taken. They had. The one destined for the children's mother contained a microdot message. Later in the day she would hand it to her husband, an attaché at the American Embassy. By the following morning it would be on its way to Washington.

Among the many items the message contained was a warning that the KGB planned a mass roundup of opponents of the Soviet régime in anticipation of President Nixon's impending 27 June visit.

The roundup was scheduled for 16 June.

Cory took possession of Parker's new identity before the middle of May. In the motel room, he sat nodding as the contents of the briefcase were shown to him and handed over one by one.

There was a passport, taken out four years before, showing a number of Western European stamps. The space for the photograph was left blank.

There was a driver's licence, a wallet with snapshots, a repair receipt ticket, and a clip of calling cards for Edward Partridge, automobile salesman. The address was in Toronto.

'It's an accommodation address,' explained the man from Technical Services, 'used by people selling cars and insurance and real estate, that kind of thing. The records will show Partridge has been on the books for two years.' He produced a sheet of paper: 'These are the places he worked before—they're all genuine but they've either closed, burned down, or the ownership has changed.'

Cory nodded. A similar list of home addresses was produced, and Cory transferred everything to his own case. 'What about credit cards?'

'That's hard,' said the man. 'The companies don't much like co-operating, and if we feed in an application, well, we turn loose an investigator.' He gestured towards the documents lying in Cory's open case. 'Those aren't bad considering the time. They'll stand up—but not to

131

too much probing.'

'That's all right,' said Cory, 'they won't get probed too much. But I still need credit cards.'

The man hesitated. 'I'll try,' he said at last.

Cory nodded. He would get them.

The following morning he introduced Parker to his new identity, and another period of learning began. At the same time Parker had to spend two hours every day talking in Russian, perfecting his accent. At unspecified times, Cory himself would shift to Russian—and expect Parker to react immediately and respond in the same language.

A week after this period of training began, Cory and Parker, travelling separately, flew into Toronto, where Parker learnt the layout of his new home town. He flew back to Washington alone. He walked out of National Airport, reluctant to take a cab immediately, eager to take advantage of his freedom for a little longer.

He had walked only a few yards when he heard a shout.

'Ed. Ed Partridge.'

He turned immediately. His false identity had become fixed. Williams was smiling; Parker had passed the test.

'Great to see you,' said the detective. 'Let me give you a lift. Car's waiting.'

A précis of the intelligence message from what was only described as a prime Russian source did not reach Sunnenden until the late afternoon of Thursday, 23 May.

He noted that the information had a high reliability rating and skimmed the information routinely until he reached one paragraph: the warning about a pending roundup of dissidents.

His face whitened with excitement. He hurried for the door, putting on his jacket as he went.

The time had come.

CHAPTER 12

Four o'clock in the morning was the bad time and even after four months there was nothing he could do about it. That was the time when Zorin felt most lonely and isolated, most depressed, most desperate.

As usual, on the morning of 25 May, he woke quickly, allowing himself no comforting half land between sleep and wakefulness. There was no light and he fumbled for the pack of cigarettes on the floor beside his bed. He could not find them—then he remembered: he had purposely thrown them out of reach the previous evening so that he would not fall asleep with a lighted cigarette.

He fought a mental battle, the need for a cigarette versus reluctance to move. At last it was not wanting to smoke that made him get up, but the feeling of emptiness beside him in the bed. He had tried to sleep in the middle, but he always woke on one side, the left, just as though Tanya was still there.

He pulled on a worn white towelling robe before turning on the lamp on the dressing table. He found the cigarettes on the floor and lit one before venturing through into the living room to heat the water for his tea.

There was a stale taste of vodka on his tongue. Drink comforted his nights until he fell asleep—but thankfully, he thought, did not tempt him in the early mornings after getting up, no matter how bad he felt. Perhaps, and this consoled him, it was another indication that deep down he was a survivor.

He made the tea and sat in one of the easy chairs to plan his day. That, he had found, was essential. In it now lay his capacity to overcome.

As soon as he awoke he became active, filling every moment until after dinner. Then at night he allowed himself to drink until he fell into sleep. It was, he thought, better and safer than pills. He might occasionally get a hangover, but never an overdose.

Today, 25 May, was a Saturday, and that in itself provided a starting-point for his planning. He had allocated each day a major undertaking. Saturday was the day to study art. He fetched a pad from his desk and carefully marked the hours from 7 a.m. until 8 p.m. In the space between 2 and 6 he wrote ART GALLERY in block capitals. The next stop was to decide not only which gallery but which particular section. That would take care of four hours. Today the decision was easy. He wanted to return to the Tretyakov Gallery to study the icons which had become one of his recent interests.

Gradually, chain-smoking and drinking tea, Zorin finished planning his day: an hour for chess, an hour for writing, the time for reading, the daily walk he would take, the shopping.

It was 5.45 a.m. when he finished. He re-read his timetable, wondering if he should change anything. Trying to get a balance was one of the pleasures: if the big event was indoors, like today's art gallery, then the walk, for example, should take him out among the greenery.

Today's walk was determined by another pre-fixed event, the bath.

After Kukhlov's initial approach in the bath house asking whether he was willing to leave Russia, there had been silence until the previous week. Then Kukhlov had hinted that something might happen soon. Today, if he read the signs right, he might be told more. Nevertheless, he tried not to let this dominate his thoughts—just in case he was wrong.

At six o'clock he began preparing breakfast. Even that

had its place in the ritual, the menu changing, though slightly, every day. Today it was cheese and cold meat and that made him feel it would be a good day. It was his favourite breakfast.

The flight for London was not due to leave until ten o'clock, but Parker was up early. He had not slept well and in the hotel coffee shop he ate quickly, conscious of edginess.

The strangest feeling was that of being by himself: apart from the flight back from Toronto he had not been alone for seven years. It was true that his freedom now was that of a dog on a very long leash.

Williams had left him in no doubt that his daughter was hostage for his behaviour once he left Washington. The threat had not been unexpected—Parker had suspected all along that his rescuers must take some precautions to ensure he did not flee once he was away from their direct control.

Even so, he had more freedom than he had had for years. He could set off for the airport when he liked, wander around London for a while, even act like any other tourist in Moscow the first few days of his visit.

It was just this freedom that frightened him—jails always held men who committed crimes simply to get back inside. Parker hoped he was not showing signs of the same dependency.

He signalled for more coffee and then drank it quickly when he realised there was a queue forming for stools.

Back in his room, with cases already open on the bed, he spent a long time looking into the full-length mirror. The change had happened gradually, but he still had not adjusted to the person who looked back at him.

The flesh-coloured skullcap that covered his thick dark hair made him look almost bald. The only hair was a fringe at the sides of his scalp. He stared closely but there was no sign of any join where the skullcap met his forehead.

The moustache was real, as was the paunch that showed above his brown trousers. Equally real, he reflected ruefully as he lit another cigarette, was the cough he had developed. His eyes were light-blue, not quite the same as Zorin's, but as near as contact lenses could make them.

He began to pack. The few items he needed to complete his conversion into Zorin were few and innocuous. The nose pads were contained in a box of ear plugs.

He packed slowly and carefully, double-checking each item even though Cory had vetted everything the previous day in Washington. The clothes were a mixture of worn and new ones. 'Everyone,' Cory had explained, 'buys something new for a vacation like this.'

Everything was either Canadian or widely available in Canada. The cases themselves, one large one and a shoulder bag that would fit under the airplane seat, were scuffed but not badly—the belongings of someone who'd had them some time but had not travelled too much or too widely. The passport conveyed the same impression.

Parker checked the folder of documents before sliding them into the zip compartment on the side of the shoulder bag. There were return Air Canada tickets to Amsterdam via London, a voucher for round-trip air charter flights Amsterdam–Moscow, vouchers for hotel accommodation in London, Amsterdam and Moscow, vouchers for sightseeing tours in Moscow, and a booklet: 'Your Vacation Questions Answered'. The last page of this was the important one: it contained Parker's itinerary. Throughout the previous evening, his first alone, he kept returning to it, even though he knew it by heart.

The Russian part of the package had been carefully chosen: Cory checked through every tour to Moscow before picking this particular one. It was listed in the brochures as lasting four days, but it offered an option, at extra cost, for tourists to stay two additional days. This would ensure Parker's returning with a different group of tourists.

At 8.30 Parker was ready to leave. He carried his own cases downstairs, double-checked the time of the airport limousine, and paid his overnight bill. He charged it to his American Express account, signing Edward H. Partridge. His hand was shaking when the cashier held it up to read the signature. Had it looked as though he was forging a name? The cashier smiled.

'Thank you, Mr Partridge,' he said. 'Have a nice day.'

By 4 a.m. on Wednesday, 29 May, Zorin was at work at his desk, the constantly refilled glass of tea within easy reach, the large ashtray in continuous use. In front of him, resting on a plain white sheet of paper, was a piece of rice paper, about four by six inches.

As soon as he was convinced he could remember everything he needed to, he would destroy the sheet. He closed his eyes and recited the lists in his head. He was certain now that he knew the details by heart, even if not what they meant. Obviously they were meeting places and times, but for whom? For him? For him and others? He had given up trying to understand. 'You want to get out,' Kukhlov had asked, and Zorin had nodded. 'Then,' Kukhlov said, 'read, learn, and we will talk again.'

The meeting was not until Friday, again at the bath house. Kukhlov had not wanted to change the pattern.

Zorin pushed back his chair, stood and began walking the room. He felt caged. He would, he realised, have to be careful. Over the months, unintentionally, he had developed clear patterns of movement and behaviour obvious to anyone who watched him long enough. Kukhlov had warned him not to vary them.

He lit another cigarette, without thinking. He found himself looking at the burning match in his right hand. He stared at the flame for a few moments and then, on impulse, picked up the rice paper and set light to it.

After three days of wandering around London, Parker was feeling more relaxed about the part he was playing. But at the same time he had grown more apprehensive about what faced him.

Despite the threat to his daughter's safety he had further debated trying to disappear. Could he make contact with his sister, get Susan moved—and then join her?

It was, he had concluded, totally unrealistic. Firstly, his sister would refuse to co-operate; even if she did, where would he take Susan and what about money? Without Cory's continued support, the papers he carried—his very identity—were useless.

Furthermore, he had no doubt that he was being watched—and would be watched until he stepped aboard the flight to Moscow.

On the night before he was due to leave for Russia, Parker stayed in his hotel room. He tried several times to write a letter to Susan, in case something happened, but at the same time not knowing whether he would ever want it delivered. He suspected that if he did not return he would prefer her to continue believing that he had just 'gone away'.

Nevertheless, the compulsion to write, to get down his feelings, to tell her what he felt for her, was overwhelming.

When he had finished, the letter covered three pages even though he was not normally good at writing. He did not read it back.

He hesitated for a long time and then wrote a short note to Cory asking him for the letter to be delivered if anything happened to him. He enclosed them both in an envelope which he addressed to Cory at the house they had occupied in Washington. He would decide tomorrow whether he would post the envelope. If he did, he had no doubt Cory would deliver the letter. Despite Williams' threat, Parker had grown to both like and trust Cory. He had even grown solicitous, concerned about Cory's air of permanent weariness; the man was obviously draining himself of more energy than his body was able to replace.

Parker switched on the television set, not knowing or caring what programme was showing, and then almost immediately called room service for sandwiches and beer.

He was surprised at the speed of the service when there was a knock at the door less than ten minutes later.

'Come in,' he yelled. When nothing happened he rose wearily and opened the door.

A hand held out an unwrapped bottle of Chivas Regal. 'Just passing,' said Cory.

They shared the sandwiches. Neither bothered to turn off the television set. The whisky lay unopened while Parker drank the beer. Cory wanted nothing.

'You've come to tell me the truth,' said Parker at last.

Cory did not answer immediately. He reached inside his jacket pocket and handed over a paper. 'As you asked,' he said, '$100,000 made out to your daughter—hers if anything happens to you.'

'And will it?'

'We'd better have that drink,' said Cory. But neither man moved.

'Tell me,' urged Parker.

Slowly and carefully Cory unfolded the plot. Then he waited. He had left briefing Parker until the moment he was sure the other could not refuse to go ahead. But he was still nervous.

Parker walked across to the television set and clicked the off switch. 'Fuck!' he said. 'I knew it had to be something like this.'

'It'll work,' said Cory quietly. 'In two weeks it'll all be over . . .'

'Fuck!' Parker hit the palm of his left hand with his right fist.

Cory's voice was harsher. 'We've got a deal.'

Parker reached for the Chivas Regal and began to uncork it. 'Yes,' he said wearily, 'we've got a deal.'

Twenty minutes out of Moscow's Sheremetyevo airport, the stewardess announced that the plane was beginning its final descent. Parker sat wedged against the window, his legs stiff from the lack of room, nursing a drink which he sipped with care because he knew the chances of getting another were small.

It was only six hours since he had last seen Cory. He had stayed with Parker most of the night, trying to still his fears. Then, after a fitful sleep, the two men shared a taxi to the air terminal.

Parker was still feeling shocked by Cory's words. The assignment had seemed hazardous enough before. But to learn that his job was to impersonate a man *and then stay behind* in Russia after that man escaped . . .

But Cory had been persuasive. There was no doubt that he had thought of everything. Parker gradually began to convince himself that, after all, even the new price was not as high as he had originally feared when he was approached in prison. Then he had suspected that whatever was involved would carry *no* chance of survival . . .

Parker closed his eyes and pictured his last sight of Cory. He had been standing across the street from the bus terminal, waiting for Parker's bus to pull out. Parker wondered why he had waited. To check whether Parker really was on board? Because he was reluctant to let go? For a moment, Parker had wanted to call out, to reassure him.

Cory had been absolutely right on one thing. Letting Parker live his role as a tourist, relaxing into his part, before telling him the full truth about his assignment, had helped.

He had begun to think of himself as Edward Partridge and constant conversation with changing travel companions on airplanes, buses, trains and in bars had helped him perfect his cover story until the answers came without any hesitation.

He took a sip of his drink. The Aeroflot TU 154A was full. Half the passengers, he had been told, belonged to some trade union group; the others were simply curious tourists—like him.

His mind kept repeating one phrase from Cory's briefing: 'and to remain behind until you hear that the man is safe' ...

The aircraft broke through cloud and Parker could see runway lights below. The plane landed with a jerk, as though it might take off again. When it finally stopped, Parker was conscious of people crowding at the windows, eager to see this alien place.

A voice somewhere behind him said, 'It looks like any other bloody airport.'

On the flight home from England, Cory began to feel guilt, triggered by what he recognised as his own unprofessionalism: there had been risks meeting Parker in London. He'd persuaded himself that such a meeting was necessary, that telling Parker the truth earlier would have been dangerously premature; and when Parker did learn, Cory needed to see his reaction.

But he only half believed himself. His real motive was the desire to be there, to be operating again. He didn't want to let go until the last moment. Now, unless something went wrong, he would hear nothing for six days. Whatever happened, it was out of his hands.

It was easier when you were your own agent, as in wartime. The personal dangers were greater, but you remained in control. It was like the difference between travelling in this 747 and piloting yourself in a small plane in a storm. Here he was safer but nervous; there he might be in danger but he was master of his own fate.

Cory had another feeling—concern. For Parker. This was not because he liked the man—although he did—but because of his young daughter.

Cory felt tired but restless. He flipped through one newspaper and then another, only to replace it in the rack and try a magazine. Two subjects seemed to dominate all of them, Kissinger's wizardry and Watergate. It was almost a month since the edited Nixon tapes had been published; almost two weeks since Nixon had said he would not resign under any circumstances.

Looking down at a photograph of the jowly face, Cory's mind searched for a word to describe the President: shabby. That was it, shabby little man . . .

Dulles was crowded: tourists flocking in. He decided against the airport bus and took a cab.

His house felt cold and empty. He had come to feel at home at the rented house with Parker and Williams although, most nights, he had not slept there.

He kicked his shoes off and walked straight upstairs.

He stood for a long time in front of the portrait of Sue.

Tomorrow he would arrange for the disposal of all the materials used to train Parker. Then there would be the fear and anxiety of the waiting followed, hopefully, by the good news.

'But what then?' he asked the picture. 'What then?'

And his hands began to tremble uncontrollably.

Now that it was happening at last, Sunnenden's great regret was that he could not talk about it with someone. There was Cory, of course, whom he had seen the day he returned from London. But Cory was acting strangely, refusing to be drawn into conversation. Sunnenden hoped that the older man was not going to break down again.

Now, on the morning of Friday, 31 May, Sunnenden received the first piece of news since Cory had told him about the London meeting. What looked like a routine cable from Moscow hid a message that there was no sign of Parker's being followed and that the briefing of Zorin would go ahead as planned.

For the moment he alone had the information; soon he would pass it to Cory, who would simply thank him and say little more. Perhaps at their meeting after Cory's return from London he had sensed Sunnenden's unspoken criticism. Sunnenden, amateur though he was, was convinced that Cory had been foolhardy to make the trip.

Nor could Sunnenden talk about it to his wife. As Cory had suggested, he had warned Janet that something was happening—something so important and so secret that he could not talk about it to anyone, not even her. That worked well at first, confirming all the effort she had invested into getting him where he was.

But now that her husband had not been chosen to accompany Kissinger on his latest Middle East tour, she was pressing for more detail, even hinting she did not believe him. Sunnenden longed to tell her the truth. Nevertheless, he would hold back until it was over. But then!

Scott was not even in Washington. To everyone's surprise he had flown out to join Kissinger in Geneva, disregarding his widely known fear of flying.

Most people believed he had gone because of Watergate: if Nixon went, would Kissinger also? And, if not, what part would he play in a new Administration? In State, it was no secret that Kissinger had dropped all his non-essential reading to study the published transcripts which were flown out to him as they appeared.

Even if Scott were here, he was even more reluctant to talk than Cory. He had made it clear that although he wished to know what stages events had reached, he wanted no details. All he cared about was results and how Sunnenden achieved them was his affair.

There were papers on Sunnenden's desk, more than usual. He was preparing a round-up of global information he thought the Secretary should have on his return. But he pushed it back, and walked to the window.

Until now it had not seemed real. Even watching Parker rehearsing his role had had a theatrical quality. The news that he was on his way to Moscow had had its own air of unreality. The information in the cable changed that. At no point had he, nor Cory, nor Scott talked about what happened *after*. Did Zorin just settle down in Israel? Could they ever talk publicly about what they had done —perhaps, one day, in his memoirs?

He just had to talk to someone—now. Even Scott would be better than nothing. He returned to his desk and pushed the intercom button.

Mrs Donovan answered immediately. 'Any news yet?' he asked. She knew what he meant. He had asked three times before: was the Secretary's aircraft on its way home?

She had never known him to be so edgy.

'No, not yet.'

'Well,' he said, 'someone must know. For Chrissake find out!'

The intercom went quiet. She stared at it for a few seconds, before picking up a phone to call the Secretary's office. God, she thought, what the hell is eating him?

The Secretary and his entourage arrived back in Washington, but Sunnenden and Scott did not talk that day.

It was, thought Sunnenden, like the return of a victorious Caesar. The Secretary's standing had never been so high. A poll of the most admired men put him firmly ahead of both the Pope and Billy Graham.

144

It was Saturday morning before he could reach Scott and by that time he had another message from Moscow: the briefing was accomplished.

The two men met at Scott's golf club. They carried drinks outside. Scott had just finished playing eighteen holes with a union lobbyist, and from his manner had played well. He looked slightly ridiculous in bright orange check trousers and a green shirt, both too tight, accentuating his excess weight.

Sunnenden cupped a hand over his eyes to stop the glare. Golf clubs made him feel uneasy; somehow, the idea of men following a small ball round a lot of greenery offended him. Golf was not even healthy—a rapid walk would have done most of the players more good.

Scott waved nowhere in particular with his free hand and said, 'Nice place, huh?'

Sunnenden lifted his glass in turn. 'I'm glad you're back.'

Scott was looking out on to the course, holding his glass aloft.

'So, tell me,' he said.

'It's go, Monday's the day. That's when our friend breaks out.'

'*Breaks* out!' Scott's voice was harsh and querulous. 'There's not going to be anything *dramatic*?'

Sunnenden felt on the defensive. 'No, no, it should all be smooth.' After a pause he added, 'You want details?'

'No, not details,' said Scott. He turned to face Sunnenden and gave a huge, politician's smile. 'Why'd I want details, when everything seems to be going well.' His voice changed, became precise. 'It is all right? No problems?'

'No problems,' said Sunnenden.

'That's what I like to hear,' said Scott.

This time his smile seemed more genuine and less forced.

'You've done good work, Bob,' he said. 'Very good work.'

He turned to face Sunnenden. 'A message for you,' he said. 'There's a meeting in the Oval Office Monday to help brief the President on his forthcoming trips to Russia and the Middle East. The Secretary would like you to sit in, help out . . .'

Then before Sunnenden could react, Scott began to laugh.

'You know what you've done?' he said. 'While we were out there screwing the Ruskies in Egypt, you've been screwing them here—right in their own yard.'

He put his arm round Sunnenden and began to lead him inside, into the bar. Sunnenden found he was laughing too. It was only later, on his way home, that he remembered there were still three days to go.

CHAPTER 13

Scott picked up Sunnenden at his office just before 9.30. 'We'll have time to walk and discuss things on the way,' he said.

Despite the heat and the fact that they had only eight blocks to walk, Scott set a rapid pace as they turned in the direction of F Street. Sunnenden found himself having to walk faster than he liked in order to keep up.

Scott did not speak until the two men stopped at the first intersection. 'I know you'll have sorted out the answers to anything you might be asked,' he said, 'but I thought maybe you ought to be prepared for what it's like in the bunker right now.'

'That bad?'

The lights changed and the two men set off.

'Can be. It won't affect anything, but I just wouldn't want you to be thrown. He rambles a little sometimes. Likes to recall things he's done.'

Sunnenden was listening, but part of his thoughts were in Moscow. Today was the day. He began to find Scott's voice, raised above the hum of the traffic, irritating. It was partly the heat, partly fatigue. He had not slept the previous night thanks to a 3.30 a.m. quarrel with Janet. She had come downstairs, understanding that he could not sleep, but angry about the glass in his hand.

And she had wanted to know what was happening. He could still hear her voice, shrill, not caring for once if the boys heard. What did he think he was doing? Why did he let everyone at State walk over him? Why was he wasting his chances? Who did he think he was fooling?

147

It had been hard not to tell her. But he had maintained a hurt silence, helped by the numbness of being semi-drunk. But God, in a few days when he *did* tell her the truth ...

Sunnenden forced his thoughts back to the present. 'So what do you advise?'

'Just remember that he's the President,' warned Scott. 'Just remember that *if* he survives, what he thinks of you matters. And that if he doesn't, Henry's going to go on—probably more important than ever.'

They turned into F Street. 'You really think he might go?' Sunnenden was surprised that Scott conceded such a possibility.

Scott paused for some seconds, as though considering the question seriously.

'For the first time, yes,' he said. 'It'll be interesting to see what happens to Kleinsdienst.' The former Attorney General was faced with being the first man in his position to be convicted of a crime in US history; the verdict was likely to be known later in the week.

'Anyway this trip to Russia is important to the President. Don't forget that. His one hope is persuading everyone that when it comes to America's position in the world he's Mr Indispensable.'

The North West Gate of the White House came into view and the two men turned into the driveway. They entered the lobby where the White House Press Corps usually congregated; the green leather chairs and couches were empty. Down the hall, they paused at a door until it was opened electronically from the other side. In another hallway, the secret serviceman nodded at Scott.

Then they were at the President's outer office and being ushered into the Oval office. The two men nodded greetings to the seven people already there. Sunnenden knew them all vaguely. Neither the President nor Dr Kissinger had arrived. One man nodded in the direction of the small green room just off the Oval office, and Sunnenden understood that Mr Nixon was there.

It was not Sunnenden's first time in the Oval office, but it was the first time that he would spend more than a few minutes.

He sat back on one of the gold sofas that stood at right angles to the President's desk. He was surprised by how little of his personality President Nixon had imposed on the room. The colours, he understood, were Nixon's choice: bright blues and golds. Beyond that the only personal touch—and a moving one—was a small presidential seal which Sunnenden seemed to remember had been embroidered by Julie Nixon.

Sunnenden opened his document case and took out a number of papers. Suddenly he became conscious of a chair being pushed back somewhere to his right. He looked up. The President was entering the room, his arm around Kissinger. The two men were still talking, heads bowed, like conspirators. Sunnenden found it hard to believe what he knew to be true: that Dr Kissinger increasingly despised the President, whom he now called 'that meatball President' in front of some of his staff.

The President took his seat in the vast green swivel chair beyond the desk. Introductions were brief; Sunnenden merited a stare and a nod. The meeting began immediately.

The various aides and officials presented short reports on the forthcoming tour: the reception arrangements in the various countries, the press contingents, résumés of the main subjects of concern ...

Sunnenden found himself awed watching the President. It was not the man, but the office, that made him feel small. Mr Nixon was, in fact, looking far from Presidential: his complexion was pallid, his face haggard. He followed the reports, though, with apparent interest, his eyes boring into whoever was talking.

Sunnenden began to feel that Scott's warnings of the President's state of mind had been overstated. Then Mr Nixon, his left knee hugged in both hands, interrupted one of his aides half way through a statement. His words were totally unrelated to anything that had gone before. With his head bent forward as though addressing his feet, the President launched into a monologue about his 'special, personal relationship' with Brezhnev.

Sunnenden looked over the room, caught Scott's eye and turned away. It was embarrassing, doubly so in view of his admiration for the man. It was like seeing a friend drunk and acting foolishly in public.

Kissinger looked embarrassed too. He kept cleaning his eyeglasses, alternating this activity with doodling on a yellow pad.

The meeting had now lost all point. The President was referring to his book, *The Six Crises*.

'I guess you've all read it,' he said. He swivelled back in the chair. 'A damned good book.'

Sunnenden began to draw squares on the top sheet of the papers stacked on the lid of his document case. The typed sheet was headed: 'Main points.'

Once or twice he thought the meeting would revert to normality, that he would be asked to present his report. He began to feel intense resentment at the chance being taken from him.

Then, suddenly, the meeting ended as abruptly as it had begun. A telephone call from an outer office reminded the President of the time. Almost in mid-sentence he stood to signify that the meeting was over.

Sunnenden got to his feet, slightly numbed at the realisation that he had not been asked to say one word. The carefully worked-on report in his hands could be consigned to the waste bin.

He thought of Janet; again he heard that hurt, angry voice. He had relied on his reports of his performance at this meeting to buy him time until he could tell her the truth. He could lie of course, but it wouldn't work; she would see through him.

The room began to empty, slowly. By his position Sunnenden found himself caught in a small group including the President, the Secretary and Scott.

The President now seemed more animated. He was joking with Scott about his passion for golf. Sunnenden looked on, wanting to join in, to speak, to say something. The President seemed reluctant to let his audience go. He was laughing at something Scott had said, his body moving in short jerky movements.

The other people had almost all left by now. Sunnenden found himself moving a pace towards the door. The President stopped him, speaking to Scott and Sunnenden.

'You guys going to be out there in the Mideast with the President?' he said, referring to himself in the third person.

He continued before either could say anything. 'If you want to do something to help the United States, you figure a way of slipping a mickey to that Meir dame. God, she's a toughie.'

Sunnenden's desire to say something, to make his mark on the meeting, could no longer be contained. Almost before he realised what he was saying, he volunteered: 'Well at least you won't have her bothering you about Alexandrai Zorin this time, sir.'

Nixon wrinkled his face. 'Who the fuck's Alexandrai Zorin?' The name obviously meant something, but he was not sure just what.

The room had gone quiet, and the voice of Leonard Way of NSC was clear. 'He's that Russian scientist whose wife was deported. The Soviets locked him in a loony bin for a while.'

Sunnenden stared down at the eagle motif on the carpet. Without looking up he knew that everyone was looking at him.

It was Dr Kissinger who spoke, his accent sharper and more Germanic than usual.

'And why won't the President be bothered about Zorin this time?'

Scott tried to intervene. 'I think if ...'

'No,' snapped the Secretary, 'let him talk.'

Sunnenden began to explain haltingly until Nixon interrupted him.

'For fuck's sake ...! Everybody but you and you out of here NOW.' He was pointing to Scott and Sunnenden. He turned to the Secretary and said briefly, 'And you, Henry.'

He waited until the rest had left the room. He was standing with his back to the desk, his hands clasped in front of him, perspiration beading his upper lip. 'Okay, now let's have the rest.'

Sunnenden was allowed to talk without interruption. When he had finished, Nixon asked the Secretary, 'You know anything about this?'

'No, sir.'

Nixon asked Scott the same question. Sunnenden only half heard the betrayal: 'I knew some, but not all this.' The voice was pained.

Sunnenden thought the bad moments had passed. Then the President exploded. 'Who the fuck employed you to do this—the Kennedy crowd? What in the name of God made you start such a shitty thing?' His hands were shaking, and his left cheek was making twitchy movements.

Nixon's voice became a low babble as he frantically thought aloud—'this on *top* of everything else that's happening. Christ, what would the press make of it. God almighty, if *this* shit ever hits the fan ...'

He made a conscious effort to pull himself together.

152

Turning to the one aide who had remained in the room, he ordered 'Joe, you personally get straight on to everyone who was here NOW and tell them they heard nothing.' He turned back to Sunnenden. 'You started this fucking thing. Now you get out there and stop it. I don't care how. Just stop it.'

He turned his back. Kissinger moved towards Scott and Sunnenden and ushered them into the outer office.

'You two, get lost for an hour,' he said. 'Then be in my office.' Kissinger turned and went back into the Oval room. The last Sunnenden saw was his back, standing next to the President, staring through the windows.

Sunnenden walked towards the street, his mind overwhelmed with nightmarish thoughts. If only he could turn the clock back fifteen minutes! What in God's name had he done? Scott was beside him.

'Why'd you say you knew nothing?' Sunnenden asked him.

Scott took his arm. 'Easy,' he said. 'You're gonna need a friend, and if I go down too, who's going to help you?'

They reached the street. Sunnenden realised he needed a drink.

Scott was wondering whether there was any way of gaining advantage from Sunnenden's outburst. Did they need to actually *do* anything? Why not let everything go ahead as planned; hadn't he already come to the conclusion that the President's days were numbered. But he quickly rejected the possibility. It had two things against it? First, it took no account of Kissinger; *he* would go on and he would not want to take any risks now. Secondly, continuing would involve Scott being knowingly implicated.

He began looking up and down the street for a cab. No, he thought, there was only one way: stop it and be seen to be the man who had done so. Sunnenden would have to drown but ...

Scott realised Sunnenden was speaking. 'What do we do?'

Anger broke in the older man. 'What the hell did you have to say anything for? Did you expect medals? All you had to do was keep your mouth shut until it was all over.'

'But what do we *do*?'

'Do? Stop the goddamned thing, that's what. Didn't you hear the man?'

Sunnenden looked at his watch. It was two minutes before eleven. Almost 7 p.m. in Moscow.

'We can't,' he said. 'It's too late.'

CHAPTER 14

For six days Parker had done everything expected of him and had even begun to enjoy himself.

He quickly established a reputation as someone who kept to himself. He attended all the planned excursions, and in the afternoons he wandered alone, a copy of the *Moscow Guide Book for Tourists* in hand. He was not being followed as far as he could tell. After four days the rest of his group had left; he kept away from the tourists who replaced them.

His fear gave way to a sense of something oddly like power; toying with a drink, he watched fellow guests and savoured excitement and pride at knowing what he alone knew. Nevertheless he continued to do all the 'right' things and none of the 'wrong' ones. He shopped—caviar, vodka, wooden dolls. He studiously bought his daily *Morning Star*, the British Communist Party newspaper. He reconciled himself to queuing as a way of life; he discussed the toilet paper with other Westerners at the bar.

He turned down the one request from a taxi driver to sell his currency on the black market and carefully avoided pointing his camera at anything that could remotely be considered sensitive.

By Sunday the second of June, a day he spent idling in the sun in Gorky Park, he had relaxed enough to begin thinking of being back in America. In the evening, as on every evening since his arrival, he practised donning his disguise: the beard he could set in place without a mirror, without showing gum. He knew he could transform himself as fast as was necessary.

That Sunday evening, though, the rehearsal was different. Looking into the full-length mirror in the bathroom, he realised suddenly that tomorrow it would be real. He lay in bed that night awake until well after three.

Could he simply not go ahead with the operation? All he had to do was—nothing. What would he do then though? Cory must have a contingency plan for just such an eventuality.

No doubt he had men available in Moscow. Someone must have briefed Zorin. And on Parker's second day in Moscow, the equipment he needed for the switchover had appeared in his room. *If* he was allowed simply to leave Russia, what would happen? Where would he go? Could he avoid being traced by Cory? Parker, remembering the way he had been released from jail, could have no doubts about Cory's long reach. Nor of his ruthlessness.

And then, there was always the threat to his daughter —something his mind tried not to contemplate. He *had* to take that seriously.

The room grew heavy with cigarette smoke. It was, he reflected, not very different from being back in his cell; only the luxury of the immediate environment had changed.

He thought then of the man Zorin: had he been rehearsing too? Was he feeling doubts? After all, he was at least alive and free—where would he be if this went wrong?

At 3.32 Parker checked his watch again, fought the desire to light another cigarette or open the bottle of gift-packed vodka, and slept.

Zorin slept well until 6 a.m. on Monday the third of June, thanks to the unaccustomed barbiturate tablet and two glasses of vodka. He felt no doubts about what was to happen, though he was reconciled to the possibility that it could go wrong. He wanted something to happen now. He was a man clutching temporary safety on a mountain side; either let him be rescued, or let him fall.

In any case he could not bear to continue living the way he had during the previous months, pretending to forsake everything he believed in. His friends put it down to an illness, a weariness of the spirit, but he knew they must talk of him, and that there must be a hardening against him every time he refused involvement in any activities.

'You must not encourage the authorities to act against you,' he had been told. At the same time, he was warned against going too far in appearing to bow before the KGB's pressures.

His head throbbed from the combination of drugs and alcohol. He lifted himself and lit a cigarette. He began coughing and, ludicrously at such a time, found himself thinking he would have to smoke less.

Parker skipped the morning tour of the Moscow Metro. That left him with the morning to fill—his carefully timed walk would not begin until the afternoon. It was to finish as the streets became dark.

He strolled aimlessly, then headed for the restaurant. By now, his standard diet was soup, meat in a thick sauce, garnished with sour cream and accompanied by *kasha*, a kind of buckwheat gruel which, prison notwithstanding, was the only food Parker had ever encountered that he could not eat.

He arrived early, but even so the meal took two hours, as always. When it was finished, he returned to his room. His two-day-old *Morning Star* was exactly as he had left it, except for the tiny blue ballpoint mark at the foot of page four. It was the message that he had waited for: the switch was on as planned.

Parker took an unopened bottle of Scotch from his suitcase and drank deeply. He corked the bottle, stripped and put on a fresh set of clothes: nondescript grey suit, white shirt, plain red tie. From the wardrobe he took an airline travel bag, marked Air Canada in large letters. Into it he placed the beard, a black beret and two plastic rings that, pushed inside his nostrils, would alter the shape of his nose to that of Zorin's. On top he placed a camera, his guide book and a light cardigan.

Parker checked his watch. Ten minutes to go, more or less, although he could always make up or lose that amount of time. He fetched a toothglass from the bathroom and poured a measure of Scotch. He drank, watching himself in the mirror of the opened wardrobe door. He placed the bottle, now a third empty, in the centre of the bed, and raised his glass to it. Not caring whether the room was bugged or not, he said 'To you and me, you crazy bastard.' He put down the glass. When he left the room it was just three o'clock.

Zorin spent the early part of the morning wandering around the flat, picking up and inspecting possessions, looking at papers, thumbing through books—things he realised he would not see again. There was much he would have liked to take, but he had decided to carry nothing away, not even a photograph.

Mid-morning he forced himself to stop and drink tea. The temptation was to begin now, but he waited an hour.

For a week the KGB had been following him spasmodically. One day no one at all had shadowed him. On two other occasions he was followed to his destination and then left alone.

Zorin suspected the reason was the extra security work necessitated by President Nixon's impending visit. Even the KGB with its vast army of men had to cut down on other work—which meant, he hoped, that he was now low on their list of priorities.

At noon Zorin turned an easy chair on its back, and

carefully began to remove, one by one, the objects hidden within. Some were wrapped in plastic bags. Kneeling, he laid them out on the floor. When he felt sure everything was there he counted to make doubly certain.

He placed all the items but six in a desk drawer that he had emptied for just this purpose. Suddenly nervous, he went into the kitchen. There was no reason for the KGB to mount a raid now, but he began to sweat even so.

In the kitchen he pinned up the close-up photograph of Parker's head next to the mirror. Over his own hair he placed a vinyl hat, like a bathing cap, which he strapped under his chin. The top was cut out, and he began to cut the hair that emerged through this hole, first with a comb to which was attached a razor blade, then, with clippers, and finally with the battery shaver.

He removed the cap. Staring back at him was a bearded monk. With the razor comb he began to thin and shape the hair that remained. It took almost an hour. Longer than he had anticipated.

Then he began on his beard, first with scissors, then the razor. This went more quickly. Twenty minutes later he tried to fit the false beard into the space that was left. He cut again until his real moustache and the false beard blended perfectly.

Cleaning up the hair was the worst part. First there was the problem of removing it from the floor where it had drifted over a wide area. Trying to brush it into a pan proved useless—his efforts only spread the fine hairs more. Finally, he had to get down on his hands and knees and painstakingly pick up hairs between his fingers, a few at a time. The task seemed endless. And then when he thought it was completed he realised bits clung to him and his clothes and also had to be removed.

The second problem was just as frustrating—getting rid of the hair. He placed a handful in an ashtray and set light to it. It flared and he thought he had found a solution. Within moments he realised he was wrong—the smell was too strong. He did not want the risk of neighbours coming to complain. At last he washed it down the sink as best he could.

By the time he had finished it was almost two. He was running late. He was not hungry, but he forced himself to eat something. He ate cheese as he worked.

Around his middle he strapped an Air Canada bag, the cardboard bottom removed, folded flat so that it followed the lines of his body. Then he dressed: a white shirt and a shapeless grey suit. He began to pack his pockets until they bulged. At last he rubbed his shaven chin with spirit.

He waited for a minute to let its drying action take effect, then smeared on the glue with his finger-tips. A tiny amount, just as he'd been taught. When he knew the glue had reached the right stage, he stretched his facial muscles and put on the beard. After a few minutes to complete the drying, he smoothed the beard and his moustache together. Even peering closely into the mirror he could see no join. The feel was strange, the look—except for the head—was not.

Time to leave. Zorin finished the cheese, standing. He put on the beret, collected the putty-coloured raincoat from the hall and, ready to leave, paused at the door, taking in the room. Whatever happened, he'd never see it again.

His eyes focused on the photograph of Tanya, on his desk, still strewn with papers as though he was just going out for an afternoon, on the pile of unwashed clothes on a chair beside the bed.

He reached for the door.

On impulse he went back into the kitchen, opened the refrigerator and took out a bottle of vodka. He uncorked it and drank from the bottle. Then, without realising he was duplicating the actions of the man with whom he was to change places, he carefully placed the bottle where anyone coming into the room could not fail to see it.

'If you make it,' he whispered, 'you'll need it.'

The day was warm and sunny. Parker turned into Marx Prospekt, joining the strolling crowds. He walked with the pronounced limp he had affected since leaving the United States. Near the trees, where the pavement was protected from the sun, the streets were still damp. Good: he would not look strange carrying his black raincoat. The coat was not essential, but it did add one further, easy item that could be used in the changeover.

He walked slowly, savouring the moment. The Scotch had lifted him without making him feel careless. Suddenly he was glad it had all begun. For one fleeting moment, he allowed himself to anticipate all this being over, his freedom, and a new life with his daughter.

He passed the Hotel Nationale. At the old home of Moscow University he turned into Hertzen Street. He passed a group of Russian tourists in front of the monument to Tchaikovsky, but then people became few. Hertzen Street had, in fact, been carefully chosen because of its comparative quiet. There was never much traffic, nor were there stores or cafés to attract crowds. It was, in short, the perfect street in which to check if you were being followed.

It was hot in the sun, and Parker looped the raincoat over the airline bag and loosened his tie. Near the end of the street he paused, leaned against a fence, and removed his shoe. He held it up, staring inside as though looking for a stone, then tapped it and put it back on. He slid the false heel-piece into his pocket. When he set off again he no longer limped.

In the week he had been in Moscow he had carefully avoided this route, familiar to him from photographs and films. As soon as he saw the Writers' House he knew what his next view would be.

As Parker left Hertzen Street and entered Uprising Square, there was a short, sudden flurry of rain—a matter of seconds, no more. The rain scurried like leaves fetched down from a tree by a sudden gust of wind, then stopped. The sun was still bright.

The square was noisy after the quiet of Hertzen Street. On his right, rebuilding was taking place: a crane held a steel pylon suspended over the vast hole that had once been a building. In front of him was a skyscraper. Even without staring he knew, from his briefings, that it was twenty-two storeys high, that it had a spire ninety-eight feet tall surmounted by a five-pointed star, and that the ground floor was a cinema and the first floor a food store.

He took a seat on a bench and began to stare at his guide-book. His reading finished, he lit a cigarette, removed his glasses, stood and walked into Krasnaya Presnya Street. He kept the glasses off.

The area was obviously an industrial district. He checked the map and made his way towards the Krasnaya Presnya Museum, passing metal working plants, a shoe factory, small engineering shops. Finally he reached his goal, 4 Bolshevistakaya Street, headquarters of the district's Military Revolutionary Committee that guided operations there during the 1917 uprising, and now a museum of the history of the revolution.

The museum had been chosen as yet another convenient point on his tour, but once inside Parker began to feel why the surrounding area meant so much to Communists. In 1905 thousands of workers had risen and fought the Tsarist soldiers. A thousand or more died. Lenin later paid tribute: 'They trained the ranks of the fighters who triumphed in 1917.'

Parker toured the ground floor; the house was almost empty. He stopped in front of one painting, a depiction of two women carrying a banner bearing the words 'Soldiers, don't fire on us.'

He looked at it for a long time, and then made for the exit. At the door, momentarily blinded by the sun, he reached into his bag and took out a black beret which he put on as he entered the street.

There had been considerable discussion as to where Zorin should spend his afternoon. Finally the National Economic Exhibition had been Sunnenden's idea. Cory agreed, liking the choice for two reasons. The first was its size: 550 acres, with nearly eighty separate pavilions. Secondly, if Zorin was followed there, he could hardly be seen doing anything less anti-Soviet.

He took the Metro, always a good way of checking whether you were being followed. He was almost sure that he was. When he transferred to the Rizhskaya Line he was certain: a small man, dressed despite the weather in a heavy dark suit. Zorin made no attempt to lose him. He had plenty of time for that.

The airline case strapped to his stomach made walking surprisingly uncomfortable. It was a relief to get on the train and sit.

Zorin walked out of the Metro on to parkland. He covered the open ground to the main entrance, aware that he was still being followed. As he entered the broad lane leading to the Central Pavilion and the start of the exhibition, he checked his watch. Just after four. He was still a little late.

In the Pavilion, he stood for a long time before the two epic canvases depicting the storming of the Winter Palace and Lenin proclaiming Soviet rule. The man following him was still there, but looking decidedly restless. Zorin wandered on.

Despite his cynicism about the wholesale propaganda of the authorities, despite his disquiet about priorities, Zorin had been immensely impressed on his only other visit to the Exhibition. He had the same feelings now, of enormous patriotism and pride.

In the main hall of the pavilion he stood in front of an electrified map of the Soviet Union showing the fantastic bounds made by every industry under every five year plan. Did people really believe it? Probably.

Zorin left the Central Pavilion and walked into People's Friendship Square, passing the two massive fountains, disregarding the pavilions around the square. He walked slowly. It would have been easy enough to lose his pursuer in the crowds but he wanted to see first whether that was necessary. If it was, he could always lose him on leaving the Exhibition grounds : then he would be 'missing' for the shortest possible time—too short, he hoped, for the KGB man even to report losing his quarry.

His beard was tickling and he resisted a desire to scratch. In front of Zorin a crowd of earnest-faced East Germans were being led in double file towards the Crop Farming Pavilion.

He entered Industry Square, dominated by a reproduction of the rocket that took Gagarin into space in 1961. As always there were groups around the base. He used them as protection while he watched the crowd. There was no sign of the dark-suited man. Good but not necessarily conclusive : he too could be hidden in a group.

The elation was dwindling when Zorin forced himself to take an interest in the exhibits. Inside the Cosmos Pavilion he wandered around sputniks, luniks, and rockets.

With perhaps forty-five minutes left before he needed to leave the grounds, Zorin took the lane to the ponds where people were fishing and boating. Although the day was hot, the grass still held dampness. He used his coat as a groundsheet and lay down, ostensibly relaxing just like everyone else. For half an hour, he ran through the coming scenario like an actor on opening night, faced with the sudden fear that he will forget all his lines.

At 5.40 he climbed to his feet and walked slowly back towards the Metro. It was here that the dark-suited man might be waiting. Zorin caught no sight of him. It was possible, of course, that they had changed tails, but there seemed no reason. Half the point of following him was to harass him, to give him constant warnings that all his actions were being observed.

Nevertheless, at Prospekt Metro station he made one unnecessary change, taking the circle line in the wrong direction for two stations before transferring and retracing his journey.

It was 6.25 when he arrived at Krasnopresnenskaya station and walked out of the train into the underground vestibule decorated with its bas-reliefs of the 1905 uprising.

On the escalator he checked his watch again: almost 6.30. Right on time. He took the bandaid from his pocket and peeled off the backing strip. As he stepped out into the street, he stuck it to his left cheek bone in the exact position he had practised day after day.

Outside the station he was sure at last. No one was following him.

He sat for a few seconds on a low wall, a tired sightseer. The false heel from his right pocket fitted easily into the palm of his hand, and he was able to locate the studs in the holes of his shoe-heel without looking. He stood and began walking slowly. The false heel, on one shoe only, made him limp—just like Parker had.

While Zorin was riding the Metro, Parker was wandering around Moscow Zoo. He hated zoos. But this one lying as it did off Krasnaya Presyna Street, was a perfect location for the final stages before the actual switchover.

He tried to make his walk take him past animals who enjoyed the maximum amount of freedom. By accident he found himself facing cages of birds ... a huge eagle lifted itself and began to rise, and where it should have soared came to land with a thump a few yards away.

For a moment he was back in his own cage.

At the large pond near the entrance he stretched out on a bench, staring at the swans and ducks and the artificial island. Gradually he felt better. He lit a cigarette, his last American one for a while, placed the pack in his raincoat pocket together with his lighter. He undid his tie, rolled it, put it in his pocket. He finished the cigarette; it was 6.30 and time to go.

As he left through the main gates he pulled the bandaid off his left cheek and dropped it into a litter bin.

From the far side of Sadovo Kudirnskaya Street, only a few paces from Uprising Square, Zorin paused. He could see the silvery cupola of the Moscow Planetarium. A trickle of people were heading towards it, making for the last programme which would begin at seven o'clock, in just fifteen minutes.

He recognised the man before he reached the entrance to the drive, but he waited until the gesture confirmed it. Parker stopped for a moment, lifted his raincoat out of the loops of the airline bag, and placed it over his left arm.

Zorin counted slowly to sixty—one and, two and, three and—before crossing the road. He paid, collected his programme and followed Parker in the direction of the cloakrooms.

In return for his coat he received a metal disc, number 17. The lavatories were beyond and Zorin saw Parker enter an empty cubicle. His instructions, Zorin knew, were to wait until there were two adjoining ones empty. Zorin hurried forward, almost forgetting his limp until he stumbled. He reached the cubicle and entered.

Zorin began to work, forcing himself not to rush. The first step was to unstrap the airline bag. Into it he placed the beret and the false beard which he tore off. He slipped on the red tie from his pocket and put on the spectacles. He ran his hand round his chin for traces of dried glue. He could find none, but as a precaution he used one of the impregnated spirit pads carried in a vacuum wrapper. Finally, satisfied, he rustled some toilet paper, flushed the chain and left.

Parker heard him go. His final steps were more difficult, more time-consuming. He worked through them methodically.

He folded the case and strapped it under his shirt. The lens turret of the camera was unscrewed and placed in one pocket, wrapped in a handkerchief, the body in the other. Then, gently, he began to ease off the wig. That went into a trouser pocket. He did not worry about the bulges; they were part of the changeover. Adding the false beard came last. Checking his face in the pocket mirror, he ran a comb through his hair and beard and moustache. Breathing heavily, he left the cubicle and went to wash.

In the gloom of the Planetarium, the two men collided, dropped coat rings, helped each other find them, apologised and found their seats.

Parker looked at his ring as he sat down. Number 17. He put it in his pocket.

In the collision he had not glanced at the other. Now, as lights began to dim, he looked around. Finally he found him. He felt a lump form in his stomach—he saw himself in the other man. Then Zorin turned in his direction. He must have been curious too.

For a few moments the two men stared at each other. Then the lights died, and the stars of a Moscow night sky glowed in the dark hall.

CHAPTER 15

The news that the switchover had been completed reached Sunnenden and Scott just before one o'clock in the morning, Washington time, on Tuesday, 4 June.

They were sitting in Sunnenden's office, Scott stretched on the sofa, a paper cup of cold coffee held in his hand.

He had fallen asleep for an hour while they waited. His head had continued whirling with the details that Sunnenden had given him about the escape plan. Now he felt even worse than before.

'Come on, Bob,' Scott said straining to keep his voice light. 'At least it means that the Ruskie don't know what's happening yet. We've still got a chance to do something before they do.'

'But what?' The question lay heavily.

Sunnenden picked up a partly-empty Scotch bottle and waved it towards Scott.

'No thanks,' said Scott vaguely. He started to say 'Go easy on the sauce,' then thought better of it.

From the outer office there was a sudden clatter from the wire machine. Scott started. Sunnenden paused from pouring his drink. 'They test at this time,' he said. Nevertheless he walked through and read the tape.

'Just in case,' he explained and returned. 'But it was testing. Just testing.'

He picked up his glass, assessed the level and added a spot more.

There was no sound now except for a slight hum from the wire machine. The only light came from two pools, one thrown on to the desk by a reading-lamp and another from the spotlight behind the sofa.

'I suppose we're certain about this,' Scott said at last.

'About the switchover working?'

'Right.'

'The arrangements for checking were pretty good.' Sunnenden noticed that he was having to speak very precisely to avoid slurring his words. He added more water to his drink before outlining the arrangements: the drunk in the courtyard of Zorin's block who would report the arrival home of the man he thought was the geneticist, the cleaner at the hotel who would note 'Parker's' return.

'They could have been turned.' Scott did not believe it himself. He was talking for the sake of it. The details of the plan had impressed him, reinforcing his anger at Sunnenden for making it necessary to try to abort it.

Sunnenden did not reply.

Scott stood and raised his hands high above his head as he stretched. 'Let's go see your friend Cory,' he said.

Sunnenden looked at his watch. It was after 1.20 a.m. 'Now?'

'Yes now,' Scott's voice was harder. 'I reckon we've got five or six hours to come up with something. Does Cory even know the switch has taken place?'

'No. I was about to phone.'

Putting on his jacket, Scott saw Sunnenden reaching out for his drink. His anger erupted. He had helped and encouraged the young man; now Sunnenden had not only blown his operation, but in so doing had negated all Scott's work. After this Sunnenden's days—and use— were over.

'And,' Scott snapped, 'for God's sake let's lay off the sauce, okay?'

The night seemed endless. Reliving it as dawn broke, Zorin could focus only on short scenes. The moment when he collected the room key at the hotel, the relief when it

169

was handed over without even a glance. The long walk to the elevator. The sight of the bottle on the bed. He had smiled at that because he knew so well what it meant—the American and he had felt a similar need to wish each other well and had conveyed it in almost identical ways.

For perhaps a half hour there had been the pleasure of activity: stripping, packing up the items of unwanted disguise, carefully rubbing a measured amount of self-tanning lotion into his beardless chin so that by morning it would not show paler than the rest of his face, and then familiarising himself with Parker's belongings. Finally there had been the ultimate of luxuries, a large Scotch drunk slowly in the bath.

But finally, and it was only eleven, the waiting began. Only once had he drifted into sleep and he forced himself out of it: the nightmares were too vivid.

Dawn was a blessing. Zorin looked down into the square, watching the old women with their cleaning brooms far below. He found some chocolate bars in Parker's case and ate one while he watched; he would save the rest to eat for breakfast instead of going down to the dining room.

At seven he began shaving, a strange sensation after years of wearing a beard. The skin where the beard had been was sore, and he winced as he pulled the blade over it.

At seven thirty, conscious that he was stretching out the time so that every moment would be filled and there would be no waiting at the end, he began to dress: checked trousers and a dark blue blazer, easily the most Western looking clothes in Parker's wardrobe. They fitted perfectly.

At eight he swallowed two more chocolate bars, debated whether to go downstairs for tea, decided against that, and drank two glasses of water.

At eight thirty he packed the single suitcase and the shoulder bag and at nine was carrying his own luggage down into the lobby to catch the airport bus with the rest of the group.

He knew what to look for: the travel agency's green and white lapel badges. Even so, he panicked at first; the lobby was so crowded with groups that he doubted he would find them without making it obvious he was not who he pretended to be.

He was saved—and given courage—at the same time.

'Mr Partridge,' she said. 'Come on, the rest are over there.'

And, smiling, the girl in the tour guide's uniform led the way towards one of the side doors.

The rest of the group were already in line, making their way into the street where the bus stood waiting. Zorin had been nervous about replying to the girl, even in his well-rehearsed whisper, but there was no need: she was busily checking off names as people boarded.

Once inside the bus, he sat, ostentatiously sniffing and holding a handkerchief to his nose. A man two seats away looked as though he was about to offer him a sweet (a cough lozenge?) and then changed his mind.

The bus filled and passersby in the street outside peered at the windows with the curiosity of those who are never going to go anywhere outside their own country.

The coach began to pull away from the kerb and there was a hum of conversation now: souvenirs were admired, experiences shared, hangovers compared.

The bus left the centre and began its journey past the dull blocks that would stretch all the way to the airport.

Zorin lit a cigarette, hardly tasting the mild American tobacco—he and his friends used to say that it was tobacco for women.

He felt himself reaching inside his jacket and fingering the edge of his passport: a strange sensation. He wanted to take it out and stare at it, examine the face that peered out.

At the front of the bus, the tour guide was speaking into a microphone, giving them instructions on how to form themselves into their respective groups and what to do when they arrived.

As the airport came into view Zorin was concentrating on his fellow passengers. Most of the talk was in English, but he heard some German and what he thought was Swedish. All would have been in Russia, what? Four, five, six days, perhaps even fourteen? Did they feel they knew the country now?

He was last out of the bus, hesitant like the rest, waiting for small groups to form, and directions to be given.

'Nothing but bloody queues,' he heard a voice say. At least someone had collected one impression. And yet it stung: he loved his country. He felt like a father; he alone could criticise his child. Now that he was going, part of him almost wanted to be caught—so that he would not have to leave.

The stream of tourists set off, zigzagging over indoor expanses of nothing, weighed down with cases, encouraged forward by the guide. They were hurrying; either they were late or the girl wanted to get away. Whatever the reason, Zorin suspected they would arrive early and have to wait.

The guide came round and did a head count: twenty-three. It was obviously the correct number. They were led off again. The next time they stopped was at the passport control point.

Zorin had positioned himself about two-thirds down the line, assuming that the border guard would spend time with the first people he saw and then, perhaps, the last.

His fellow tourists began fumbling for their passports. A couple a few yards in front of him were having difficulties; finally they found them in a carrier bag. Zorin could not comprehend how anyone could be careless with such a precious possession.

They shuffled forward until, after twenty nerve-racking minutes, it was Zorin's turn. He handed over the passport. For what seemed an eternity the guard studied the pink visa page containing Parker's photograph. Then he ripped off the sheet, handed back the passport and barked 'Next.'

Zorin hurried through, scurrying to catch up with the previous tourists, desperate for the protection of the group. The first hurdle was over.

The second was more nerve-racking, because it took longer and because he was forced to answer questions.

'This your camera?' asked the official who was checking his case. The question was asked in Russian.

Zorin forced himself to look blank and lost. With a gesture bordering on despair, the official repeated it in English.

Zorin nodded and whispered 'Yes.'

He wanted to smoke but dared not. Even if his hands did not tremble, he feared that the simple act of lighting up might look suspicious. The official emptied half the case. He held up a shirt, tossed it back into the case, unfolded, and turned away to talk to a colleague behind him.

Zorin waited.

The official turned. 'All right,' he said. 'Go. Go.'

Zorin piled the belongings back into the case, zipped it and passed into the departure hall without looking back.

Suddenly he *knew* he was safe. Oh yes, much could happen still, but his fears had gone. They were replaced by a kind of numbness. Take-off meant nothing. He did not bother to lean over to stare out at Moscow as it unfolded below him.

He sat immobile for perhaps an hour, seatbelt still fastened. Then automatically he reached out and took the newspaper the stewardess was distributing. The words

173

were a jumble; suddenly he began to shiver and his eyes filled with tears.

Parker spent the morning of Tuesday, 4 June looking through Zorin's apartment.

He was not searching for anything in particular, he was simply curious. From the moment he had seen Zorin's face, he had wanted to know more about him.

In Washington he had studied Zorin, read his psychological profile, watched the films of him walking and sitting and climbing steps, heard tapes of his voice, read translations of his words ... But, now Parker felt that, despite everything, he did not know him at all.

The search did not help much. Just three things gave Parker a brief feeling that he might see something of the real man. There was the opened bottle of vodka, placed where he would be sure to see it. But that spoke more of Zorin's mood at the time he had done it—Parker, after all, had done roughly the same thing. Then, there was the photograph of Tanya. Her face itself did not interest Parker. What did was the fact that Zorin had left the picture behind. He would have been told to take nothing, of course, but the photograph was surely a favourite one. Parker himself would have taken it.

And thirdly, there was a game that was in progress on the chessboard. It was a game he recognised, a good one to re-enact because of its twists and excitements. But it was an odd one for Zorin to choose at a time like this.

As an avid chess player Parker knew that, notwithstanding what many people believe, luck can play a part in chess.

This game was known as 'Steinitz's missed immortal,' played back in the 1880s. Its great interest lay in the fact that the player who should theoretically have won had pursued a policy of sacrificing pieces in order to ensure his final victory—but had, in fact, lost the game because of precisely the element of bad luck.

Mid-morning, sitting straddled across a chair facing the photograph, Parker was not sure what inference he could draw from it all. That Zorin was a hard man, a survivor? That he was conditioned to obey orders? That he was so anxious to get out that he would not risk the smallest thing?

Parker wandered back to the chessboard, picked up a queen and took a rook.

Did the chess game reflect Zorin's fear? Or was Parker reading too much into too little? Perhaps it was the quiet, the isolation of the apartment. Like all old buildings this one was full of noises. Each time its brickwork contracted, or a door on another floor closed, he listened at the door: if anyone called he could only hope and bluff. He had become resigned to the waiting, but he wanted afternoon to come.

At lunchtime he finished the vodka, ate the rest of the cheese, and double-checked that the radio was tuned to the right wavelength for *Voice of America*.

At 2.10, as planned, the sound of *Getting Sentimental Over You* filled the apartment. There was a little vodka left in his glass and Parker toasted the radio set. Zorin was in Amsterdam now. It was time to go.

Outside, in the courtyard, he kicked aside an empty bottle and noted the KGB car parked across the street. This was almost the final test. If no one stopped him here he should be safe.

He turned right out of the courtyard and joined the thin stream of people heading towards the main streets. He saw an empty cab and wanted to take it, but that would have been out of character for Zorin. He walked.

Throughout the afternoon—an hour's walking, two hours in a cinema, a half hour in a cafe—he was conscious of his shadow.

At six he walked to a bus stop, having no idea where it

was going. The bus arrived; he got on, pushed his five kopecs into the machine and took a ticket.

Two stops later he saw a Metro station. He waited until the last moment, until the bus doors had begun to close, and forced his way through the crowd.

The doors were almost closed when he reached them; he pushed his shoulder through the gap and heaved. Behind him he heard mutters of reproach; the Russians do not like people who step out of line—and what he took to be the sound of his tail trying to elbow his way through. Then he was outside and hurrying through the crowds to the Metro. He walked quickly down the escalator, overtaking shoppers making their way home. Near the bottom he looked back. He was clear.

Nevertheless he took the Metro three stops, came up into the open again, walked and took another Metro before making his way to his destination, the New Cherry Trees station.

He emerged from the station to a vista of skyscraper apartment blocks, all identical. On foot, Parker found them even more impersonal and depressing than he had done from the tour bus. He remembered the Intourist guide's proud words: 'And only twenty years ago there was nothing here but fields and villages ...'

The buildings were surprisingly far apart and it took him over a quarter of an hour to reach the third block. By now it was dark. A taxi arrived just ahead of him and deposited a man with a briefcase. Parker waited a few seconds and followed him into the entrance.

Although there were elevators—and only one was marked 'Out of Order'—the man had taken the stairs. Parker waited and then did the same; Russian lifts had a way of stopping inexplicably; he did not want to have to be rescued.

He walked up four dark flights, and then pushed his way through a barrier door. Number 49 had no name, only a bell push. He pushed it once and then again a few moments later before concluding that it did not work. He banged with his hand.

Still there was no reply. He rapped with a coin. He began to worry. At best, no one was at home, even though someone should have been. At worst, the occupant had been arrested. Then the door opened.

The woman had a towel around her head. She was perhaps forty-five, small and stoutish, her round, high bosom confined in a frilly shirt.

Two buttons were undone and Parker realised that she had been stripped to the waist. Washing her hair. Despite the situation, he felt a stir of excitement.

'Well?' said the woman.

Parker remained silent, tongue-tied.

'Well?' This time there was a frown.

Parker took off his beret and clutched it to his chest with both hands like a servant calling on a master. 'I am Josef's cousin's friend,' he said at last.

'You'd better come in, then,' she said, expressionless.

As he entered, she peered down both lengths of the corridor. She followed him in and closed the door. Parker was still standing, beret clutched to his chest, feeling clumsy, a little embarrassed, like a teenager on a date.

Then the woman reached forward and took his hand. Before he realised what was happening she had lifted it and kissed it.

'Thank God you made it,' she said.

CHAPTER 16

Cory was asleep when Scott and Sunnenden reached his house. He had stayed awake until after one o'clock and had then drifted into sleep.

At first he thought that the ringing of the doorbell was the telephone and, half awake, he fumbled for the instrument. He lifted it and muttered 'Hello', but the ringing continued.

There was water in a jug on a coffee table, alongside a near empty glass of whisky and water. The ice had melted. Cory poured some on to his hand and rubbed it over his face. He drank the rest from the jug and made his way, still unsteady, to the front door.

He watched the two men through the peephole first. Sunnenden was pacing forwards and backwards in a few square feet of space, and the other man was rubbing his hands.

He knew at that moment that something was wrong. He took them into the kitchen and began heating coffee. He recognised Scott, but did not ask what he was doing with Sunnenden; he must be one of the 'principals' that Sunnenden had referred to. 'They've been caught?' he asked.

'No,' said Sunnenden, 'nothing like that. One's out and as far as we know the other's okay.'

Cory was puzzled now. 'So what's wrong?'

They told him.

The three men talked for almost four hours, perched on stools in the kitchen, drinking countless cups of coffee, watching daylight arrive and Washington awake.

Although Sunnenden knew what had been planned for Zorin and Parker once the switch was complete, and he had told Scott, only Cory knew all the details.

Now sadly and carefully Cory spelled them out. Zorin was to stay in Amsterdam for just under forty-eight hours during which time he would be debriefed unofficially. That was Cory's contribution towards repaying the CIA's clandestine department for their help. Parker was to remain in Zorin's apartment until he knew the geneticist was safe. He would then move to an apartment on the outskirts of the city, where he was expected, until it was time for him to present himself at the American Embassy. There he would explain that he had got drunk, been robbed, and only wanted to return home.

'The idea,' said Cory, 'is that even if no one believes us, it's in everyone's interest to get him home. Nobody gains anything by making noises.'

Scott poured more coffee into a mug, emptying the pot. Cory took it from him and began making more. His method was simple; he made coffee the way English make tea—by spooning coffee into a pot, covering it with boiling water, then letting it stand. Scott and Sunnenden watched, pretending to be more absorbed in the process than they were.

The coffee made, Cory refilled his own cup and Sunnenden's.

Scott began asking questions: when was Zorin to be approached and by whom? What was the apartment that harboured Parker? When was he to leave? Were the embassy expecting him?

Almost perceptibly he began to take command. If the situation were to be salvaged, he felt he had to. Sunnenden was obviously useless. And although Cory was reacting professionally, Scott doubted the man's mind could easily come up with a scheme that would destroy his own plans.

In the long silence that followed the questioning, his mind grasped ideas, only to reject them one by one.

Cory was the first to speak. His voice was so low that Scott was not sure he had heard it right. He asked Cory to repeat it. This time there was no mistake.

'We could always tell the Russians.'

'What the hell for?' said Sunnenden, his voice full of puzzlement.

Cory made as though to reply, but Scott stopped him with a gesture. He understood. He had toyed with the idea.

'Could you handle it?' he asked Cory.

Cory stared at the table, his expression blank. At least he could save Parker. He looked up, straight into Scott's eyes.

'Yes,' he said quietly and firmly. 'I could do it.'

The envelope had been left at the Information desk, just outside the Customs area at Schipol Airport. It was addressed to J. K. Zak, and inside there was a key.

Zorin placed it carefully in his pocket and took the airport bus to Amsterdam terminus, behind the railway station. The key, as he knew it would, opened a left-luggage compartment. Inside was a manilla envelope, containing a single sheet of paper bearing the name of a hotel—the Red Lion—a telephone number, and a new passport.

Cory had thought that Zorin should switch to a different name at this point—just in case something went wrong in Moscow, and the KGB began looking for an Edward H. Partridge. The name in the passport was Leonard Rose.

He took the passport and the paper, placed his old passport in the now empty envelope and closed the compartment, leaving the key inside. In a near-by lavatory, he memorised the hotel name and the telephone number, and tore the sheet into strips before flushing it down the pan.

He left the station, weighed down with weariness, exhausted by strain and tension.

It was the first time he'd seen Amsterdam, but the view that faced him was exactly the way he knew it would be: the boats and bridges, the trams clustered together, and the cyclists.

There was a queue for cabs. Rather than wait, he decided to walk, notwithstanding the tiredness. He sought the haven of the hotel.

Ahead of him lay the Damrak. He crossed the street and started up the city's only real boulevard, with its wide pavements and terrace cafes.

The heat was getting to him now. He wanted to stop, to drink a beer, but he forced himself to keep going on until he reached the hotel.

'You look,' said the counter clerk, checking the reservation list, 'like a man who could do with a long, cold drink.'

It was almost eleven. Cory had been too involved making arrangements to eat dinner, but now he was so exhausted that he did not want food.

Alone in his house, he was torn between a need for valium and the desire for a drink. He decided on the pill, made lemon tea, and settled down in the study room overlooking the street.

There were spaces on the long table now and he positioned himself by one of them, setting down a notepad and a soft lead pencil and then, neatly beside them, the glass of tea.

The valium was already beginning to work. He would be no good for anything within half an hour. He thought he had done it all but, like a man going on vacation worrying over unlocked doors and running taps, he needed to check again.

He began to write on the pad.

1. Cancel debriefing. Arrange delivery Zorin Amsterdam-Tel Aviv air tickets 6 June flight.

By that he put a tick.

2. Arrange delivery Moscow agreed story.

3. Arrange back up diplomatic approach: Washington Amb?/Moscow Ambassador?/Hot line (S. fixing).

He went on through the list, the words written in large, careful, almost childish writing. The plan was basically simple.

He had arranged for the Americans to tell the Russians that the CIA had stumbled across a plan to free Zorin, but too late to do anything about it. They did, however, know where he was located. As a further mark of America's good faith and belief in détente between the two great nations, they were passing on the information.

The blame would be placed on a Western-based right-wing private escape organisation. There was one—operating in West Berlin to bring out men from East Germany —that for some time had been an embarrassment to the Americans and to West German intelligence.

The great strength of the plan was that it did not matter whether the Russians believed the story or not. They would pretend they did and take appropriate action. It was in their best interests.

At 2 a.m. on Wednesday, 5 June Parker awoke with a convulsive shiver.

He lay, sweating, taking in for a few moments the dark room, no light at all.

It frightened him. In prison he had longed for darkness, but this blackness was too much.

He was lying wrapped in one blanket on two chairs pushed together. His feet were drawn up, but he would have been comfortable enough without the fear.

For a while the only sound was that of his own heart

and then, finally, he heard the woman's breathing, soft and shallow. He could not see her but he knew her bed was in the far corner, a convertible settee that, opened, half blocked the door into the only other room, the kitchen.

Her name was Anna and she worked at one of the government offices. Beyond that he knew only that Cory had told him she was safe. He could tell her nothing, of course. She had her story, said Cory, and that was enough.

As it was, she had asked only what she should call him. Before he could answer even that she had added, 'No, don't tell me, I will call you Kurt.' Was it just a name, or did it mean something?

Parker pinned his thoughts on her to keep away the panic. After the first unexpected gesture of kissing his hand, she had been motherly and solicitous.

They sat at the kitchen table, she encouraging him as he ate a plate piled with canned herring and cheese and hard-boiled eggs with hunks of black bread.

With it, she gave him Pertsovska vodka, flavoured with red peppers. He gagged on the first mouthful. 'No,' she said, 'let me show you.' She demonstrated how 'real Russians' drank vodka—pour a small glass, breathe out, swallow in one gulp, wait, then breathe in.

They both began to laugh and just as Parker was thinking that she looked almost pretty, the woman's face became stern. 'I shall put you to bed. Tomorrow I must be out early.'

Parker had fallen asleep immediately, his lullaby the sound of her washing dishes, and then, in his half sleep, the noise of her converting the sofa into a bed.

He levered himself on to his elbow and tried to make out the time on the luminous dial. He thought it said 2.10. He fell back and the chair creaked.

In the silence that followed he heard the woman move in her bed. Then there was a voice: 'Do you want to come into bed with me?' she asked. Her voice was a monotone.

Parker waited some time. It might have seemed that he was considering it. He was actually trying to draw strength to speak.

'Yes,' he said finally. 'Yes I do.'

Two meetings between American diplomats and Russian officials took place in Moscow on Wednesday morning, 5 June. The first was in the formal surroundings of the Soviet Foreign Ministry, the huge yellow skyscraper a few blocks from the American embassy.

In the short ride to Smolenskaya Square, the US Ambassador rehearsed his briefing in his mind. He had been wakened early at his Residence and told that there was an 'Ambassador's eyes only' cable waiting at the embassy. He read it later with growing apprehension and anger. Ambassadors were often used as messenger boys—but to carry a message like this!

Arranging the meeting had been easy. Often days could go by, but from the reception his call had received it was obvious that the President had already made contact with Brezhnev.

Much though he hated the mission, the Ambassador was a professional. For nearly thirty minutes he sat in the Soviet Minister's office, reading aloud the *aide-mémoire* he had put together in the brief time before the meeting.

The Minister said nothing. The American Ambassador could not tell from his eyes whether he believed the story or not.

Finally, the reading finished, the Ambassador handed over the *aide-mémoire*. There was a pause during which he had a sudden fear that it would be refused. Then, again without any show of emotion, it was taken from him. Moments later he was being ushered to the elevator.

The second meeting, unknown to the Ambassador or

the Minister, took place rather less formally on the banks of the Moskva River.

The Russian arrived first and was sitting on a bench when the American came into view. They began walking immediately.

The two men had a guarded respect for each other. Such a feeling was essential. When they did meet—and there had been only two previous occasions—it was because it was in the interests of both their Services.

The Russian, a solid man with a strange habit of swinging both arms in the same direction as he walked, wore a dark blue suit.

The American was almost a caricature: cropped hair, rimless spectacles, a square face, button-down shirt.

The American began talking, knowing that his voice was probably being recorded, either by a microphone concealed on the Russian, or by a parabolic microphone on one of the boats that plied Moskva. He spoke slowly and carefully. He did not want the tape to get anything wrong. He was not sure whether the Russian would have the power to make decisions on this matter alone.

Occasionally the Russian interrupted to ask a question, but mostly he was quiet. As the story ended, they stopped and turned to face each other. The Russian crossed his arms across his chest.

'And that is all?' he asked.

The American nodded.

The Russian thrust out his hand and shook the American's. Then, without a word, he turned and walked away.

As the American expected, the story invented by Cory did move upwards, to Andropov, the KGB chief, from his contact and as a memo to the Politburo from the Minister.

Andropov dropped by during the afternoon to chat with Brezhnev in his Kremlin office next to the Politburo room. He was not in the austere room itself, but in the small room behind what appeared to be a built-in cabinet. Andropov, one of Brezhnev's closest friends, was one of the few who saw him in this hideaway where he went to nap, rest, or watch television.

Like everyone else involved, they agreed the story was basically untrue. Like everyone else, they agreed it was in their interests to pretend they believed it. There was much to gain, nothing as far as they could see to lose. The Americans had done something stupid; the Russians would remember, but for now the mistake worked to their benefit.

That evening the American received a brief telephone call, the substance of which was no more than the expression of thanks. He set off for the embassy to send the cable that would signify that the Russians were prepared to accept the story.

What the American did not know was the news coming into the KGB centre, even as he sent the cable. There had been raids in West Berlin late the previous night on the homes of members of an organisation that specialised in smuggling men from East to Western Europe. Two smugglers were dead and, according to the report, there were indications that their organisation had been turning its attention to Russia itself.

Zorin stayed in his room overlooking Damrak until mid-afternoon.

At five he risked a brief excursion—no further than a pavement café a hundred yards from the hotel. He sipped his beer and chain-smoked Disque Bleu, which he liked better than the mild American brands.

It was pleasant in the sunlight and he took his time, drinking slowly and enjoying the easy atmosphere of the crowds around him.

Reluctantly, just before six, he left money for the bill,

pushed his way through other tables and started back along the street.

'Stop!'

The command was in Dutch but there was no mistaking the meaning, nor the fact that it was meant for him.

Zorin froze. His heart pounding, he turned.

A hand was already reaching out to grasp his shoulder —a policeman.

It was, Zorin realised, all over. Something had happened.

Then he became aware of the policeman's face: he was smiling. The policeman was pushing something at him with his free hand.

The policeman spoke in the universal tourist language, English.

'Your lighter,' he said. 'You left it on the table.'

CHAPTER 17

Considering the speed at which they had been made, the arrangements were elaborate. Kovalev left The Hague's Central Station and tried, unsuccessfully it seemed, to make a telephone call from one of the boxes in Koningin Juliana Place. Leaving, he dropped a handful of change.

The young man who helped him retrieve it was talkative. 'One is always clumsy after a long journey.'

Kovalev's Dutch was slow but adequate. 'Tiredness and clumsiness are bedfellows.'

The boy walked off, and Kovalev watched him pass a parked Daf, smoothing his hair as he went.

Kovalev picked up his case and walked toward the Rijn Straas. It was hot and he was glad when the Daf pulled up beside him and the passenger door opened.

The drive, conducted in silence, lasted little more than fifteen minutes. During the last few of them Kovalev, watching the interior mirror, saw a small van following. In an empty side street it passed and stopped. The Daf pulled up close behind. Kovalev transferred to the back of the van. It pulled away almost immediately.

The driver talked without looking round: 'I was told to apologise that you were not welcomed in a more dignified way, but you would understand when you saw the embassy.'

'I know it,' said Kovalev in a tone that signified he did not welcome conversation. He lay back against the side of the van.

Kovalev was a big man, over 220 pounds. His face seemed to be permanently on the verge of a smile. There were laughter lines around his eyes. Given a beard, he would have made an excellent Father Christmas. It was obvious that he was one of life's jolly fat men.

Despite the discomfort, fatigue and puzzlement about why he had been ordered to get to The Hague as quickly as possible, he genuinely found the situation amusing. He outranked most ambassadors, and here he was being delivered in an old Citroën van like a sack of groceries. But then he had never wanted the trappings of power, only the reality. Perhaps this was the reason he had outlived not only the war, but Stalin and that oaf Khrushchev and Beria and all the changes *his* going had meant.

There was also something more than amusement: an excitement he had not felt for years. These days he was a manipulator, a manager, not a field operative. The previous weeks had been spent in Portugal trying to guide the April coup in the 'right' direction, so that the country would become Europe's Cuba. When he had been intercepted only three hours before, he had been in Brussels on his way to a meeting with European terrorist leaders. He did not know why he had been diverted to Holland, only that it was urgent and obviously important. It felt, though, like being back in the front line again after all these years of directing others.

His war had been full of moments like that from the time when, as a seventeen-year-old, he had fought behind the lines with the partisans. It had never ended, only changed. After 1945 he had stayed on, until he had been asked to help train foreign guerrillas at the camp at Simferopol in the Crimea.

The driver interrupted his thoughts. 'We'll be there in about five minutes. Please lie low—there's always a watch on the gates.'

Kovalev had three qualities that made him attractive to the KGB.

He had a seemingly insatiable curiosity and interest in

the mechanics of death. To this end, he had always read and sought out experts in various fields from pathology to chemistry.

He saw life as permanent warfare. Like Mao he believed that 'war cannot for a single moment be separated from politics, politics are bloodless war, war is the politics of bloodshed.'

And, perhaps above all, he could not understand false sentimentality about death. Thousands of people died every hour. To kill, in peacetime, was simply an extension, on a very small scale, of what was acceptable in war; scores compared with millions.

'Just two minutes,' warned the driver.

Kovalev wedged himself diagonally across the van, feet pushed against the rear corner, anticipating that the driver would make a sharp turn.

'Get ready,' instructed the driver. 'Almost at the turn.'

Kovalev braced himself and felt the van turn sharply. Lying as he was, he could see the mound of his stomach. The van stopped only a few paces from the side door of the embassy. It was not big by diplomatic standards. The building, a typical old colonial house, stood at the end of a thirty yard drive. Inside there was marble and mahogany panelling. The coolness was a relief after the heat of the van. Kovalev took several deep breaths and began to follow the driver, first up one flight of stairs and then along a corridor. There was total silence; they could have been alone in the building. They made their way through two doors, one with an entry phone and the other with a peephole, into the Referentura, that area of a Soviet Embassy occupied by the KGB.

Kovalev had experienced many of them. All were unpleasant—no daylight because windows were sealed and cemented over as protection against outside surveillance, and stale air because there either was no air-conditioning or it was inadequate.

Here the Referentura comprised six interconnected rooms. Kovalev passed through two outer ones, manned by a half-dozen clerks and secretaries looking as bored as office workers anywhere.

They reached the inner suite. Again the door was steel. Once through it, Kovalev was struck by two things: the hum of the coding machine which, for some reason, gave off a permanent whine, and the sickly pale faces of the clerks, who were allowed during their terms of duty to leave this confined world only under guard.

Sakulkin was waiting. He stood while Kovalev entered. His face was deeply tanned and he looked in good condition. When they shook hands Kovalev was conscious of the softness of his skin. Without doubt, he was one of the new breed of men recruited by the KGB since the late 1950s in order to present a better image abroad. Sakulkin's welcome was warm, yet formal. Despite his youthful confidence, the overweight, crumpled visitor with his folds of chin and perspiring face made him uncomfortable.

Kovalev launched straight into business. 'Do you know what all this is about?'

The younger man handed him a sheet of paper. Still standing Kovalev read it quickly. 'This arrived when?'

'Just under four hours ago.'

The sheet contained a coded message from Moscow ordering Sakulkin to place an American staying at the Red Lion Hotel under immediate surveillance. It described the man and notified Sakulkin that Kovalev was on his way by train. Arrangements to meet him and bring him to the embassy were to be made with the greatest secrecy possible.

The last line emphasised that Kovalev was to be given all help short of jeopardising Soviet intelligence operations in the country. Kovalev smiled inwardly at the phrasing; it was to ensure that if Sakulkin made a decision that proved wrong, it was the younger man's head that would fall.

Kovalev handed the sheet back to Sakulkin ... 'There's more?'

'This.' Sakulkin handed over a second sheet still in cipher. Only Kovalev could decipher it.

'I'll need a room,' he said.

Sakulkin led him into the soundproof conference room. 'I'll be outside,' he said and left Kovalev alone. Kovalev pulled back a chair, slid over paper and pencil. Then he took a packet of cigars from his breast pocket, removed one and carefully peeled away the outer layers of leaf until a slim band of white paper emerged. It contained letters in groups of five digits. It was a one-time pad, the system of ciphering and deciphering in which each letter is represented by a new symbol every time it appears— unbreakable by anyone other than the sender and the man with the pad.

Using the pad, Kovalev decoded the message. His face betrayed no feelings, but his fingers began to tingle the way they did when a storm was brewing. The message told him the 'American's' identity, informed him that files on Zorin were on the way from Moscow, and gave him details of the man's flight plans for the following day. The rest of the message was couched in the same officialese, but it was what made Kovalev's fingers tingle: 'Action: terminate. Method/time/place, operative full control.'

Kovalev looked at his watch. Just before six o'clock in the evening. He had eighteen hours before Zorin flew out of Schipol airport.

Kovalev held a match to the sheet of the one-time pad. Made from cellulose nitrate, it flared immediately and became powder. To cipher or decipher other messages Kovalev would use another, different sheet, taken from another cigar.

He lit another match and set light to the message itself.

There was a knock on the door. Kovalev barked, 'Enter.' It was Sakulkin. 'There's a special pouch delivery for you,' he said.

Kovalev followed him out and through two rooms until they reached a small photographic darkroom. The package, delivered by diplomatic courier, would be the file on Zorin.

Kovalev nodded appreciatively. At the Center they knew that he would want detailed copies of reports together with photographs—not just radioed information. And they had despatched the material as soon as he was diverted to The Hague. Kovalev watched the package being opened. Inside the bag was a black canister, about nine inches in diameter. The top was screwed on, and, ostensibly, needed only to be turned to be removed. The clerk placed over it a paper disc with markings round the rim and turned the top of the canister backwards and forwards so that a solitary mark on it coincided with a sequence of numbers on the disc. It was, Kovalev knew, operating exactly like the combination of a safe. Unless the exact sequence was carried out before the lid was removed, a capsule of acid would break, destroying the contents.

Finally the lid was removed and rolls of film were lifted out.

Kovalev stood in the miniscule darkroom as they were developed. The processor's face was red in the darkroom light, and Kovalev found himself wondering how anyone could live as these men did, like caged animals, eating, sleeping, relaxing, talking, for months on end in these confined and cheerless quarters. Even prison allowed a man more dignity.

The processing was swift. Using high activity developer at a high temperature the films took less than a minute to develop. They were then projected through the enlarger on to special paper that contained the microscopic capsules of developer needed to produce a print. The paper was passed through hot rollers, bursting the capsules and liberating the solution.

Kovalev collected the dry prints as they emerged and waited to watch the negatives destroyed. He returned to his table.

The information on Zorin was divided neatly into sections under headings such as Family and Physical and Contacts. In addition there were notes, fairly crude despite the medical jargon, by a psychiatrist who had, it seemed, witnessed parts of an interrogation. Kovalev read the details quickly and then again slowly, pausing frequently.

He needed to know his man. He believed that just as men live according to patterns, so do they die in ways that make their relatives and friends and workmates nod as though they knew all along that this was the way young Boris or old Josef would go. The drinker falls downstairs, the heavy smoker has cancer or suffers a heart attack, the perpetual dreamer steps under a bus ...

He read for a third time, skimming frequently. Time was his greatest problem.

The message from Center left him free to determine how and when the killing should take place, but he had no doubt they would prefer Zorin's death to seem either accidental or natural.

His mind raced through possibilities: a street accident, an overdose in a hotel room, a fall from a window ...

Zorin was due to leave the following day on the 11.30 flight to Tel Aviv.

The airport gave him the great advantage of the maximum time in which to make arrangements. From experience he also knew that airports were good places to arrange accidents. The assassin is hidden by the crowds of people; rush and strain frequently bring on heart attacks; and airport staff are geared to hushing up un-

194

pleasant incidents as quickly as possible. Corpses are bad publicity.

The airport then, but where and how?

The idea came to him swiftly. He went outside the room and found Sakulkin. 'Flights from Schipol to Tel Aviv,' he said. 'You have files?'

'I'll bring them.' At least, thought Kovalev, the younger man was efficient.

He began reading as soon as the files arrived. He quickly noted the parts that interested him.

All Tel Aviv flights from Schipol left from the end of C pier, so that before every flight the area could be completely sealed off and searched. Passengers were then let in and checked one by one before being allowed to step on to the bridge and into the plane.

There were two different police forces at the airport. The Marechaussee conducted immigration checks and patrolled the runways. And the State police, Kovalev's immediate concern. These men, under the Minister of Justice, supervised the checks on the passengers.

He finished reading. Difficult, he thought, but it could be done. He checked his watch again—just seven o'clock —and review his idea quickly, looking for flaws. He could see none, only the problems of time.

Having got this far, he knew the Center would expect him to give directions to Sakulkin and then stay in the background, monitoring.

He found himself envying the man who would put the plan into operation. But what had his instructions said? 'Operative, full control'.

What if he decided to handle things himself?

He imagined the excitement of being back in action, of personally manipulating things move by move. That would show the soft newcomers like Sakulkin and his equivalents back home!

Why not! Who, after all, was better equipped? Who

had his background? He wasn't past it despite the things he knew some of the newcomers whispered.

He made his decision.

Quickly unpeeling another one-time pad, he sent a terse message to Moscow. The reply came less than an hour later. He tried to doze while he waited, knowing he would have little or no sleep until this was over.

The reply was in two parts. The first confirmed that a non-metallic bomb was on the way from the Soviet mission in Dublin, the nearest KGB 'store'.

The second said simply, 'Van Louden, H-154321. Michael's brother Petri'. It was too secret a message for anyone else to see, even the Resident.

154321 was a Hague telephone number. 'Michael's brother Petri' was how Kovalev should introduce himself. Van Louden was the name of the Soviet spy who headed Russia's illegal network in the Netherlands, planted so deep that even the resident agents at the embassy had no knowledge of his identity.

Van Louden would supply an assassin.

It was 9.27 when Kovalev turned out of the railway station and walked in the direction of the houseboats. The address he had been given was a fifteen-minute rail journey from The Hague. The short trip had given him a chance to think calmly.

The houseboats were moored at a point where the canal ran parallel to the railway track. As he neared, Kovalev saw their sameness; all were white, all with a small garden on the bank, and on the roof of each of them an identical TV aerial.

Kovalev did not know Van Louden's real identity even now. He did know from his work for the Center that one of Van Louden's major jobs in Holland was infiltrating the various Palestinian organisations. This had been a major Soviet preoccupation since 1968, one that intensiied as the country's standing in Egypt had declined.

Kovalev wanted one of Van Louden's Palestinian sympathisers to carry a bomb on board Zorin's flight. It would be written off as just another Palestinian attack. Zorin would die and Russia would be blameless.

But first Kovalev needed Van Louden's co-operation. It was no good getting the Center to issue an order—Van Louden's position was so strong that if he had any reservations about such an instruction he could, at the very least, cause delays. And time was something that Kovalev did not have. That was why he wanted to see Van Louden face to face.

He reached the first houseboat and began counting: he wanted the eleventh. He reached it, checked for a bowl of red tulips in the left corner of the window, then walked across the plank. The door was open. Inside, it was dark after the sunlight and he felt a brief wave of panic. He could hear nothing except the creak of wood as the boat shifted slightly in the water. He was getting old and it was too long since his operational days. Once he would never have stepped through a door like that.

A man stepped forward into his vision. They stared at each other. Even after all these years, and with all the changes, Kovalev recognised him instantly. The two men began to laugh.

'Jan van Louden,' said Kovalev as they embraced, 'you are the finest Dutchman I have ever met.'

'And you, my friend Petri, are the finest Fritz,' said Van Louden. Kovalev, he knew from the message from Moscow, was travelling on a German passport.

Van Louden went through into the galley and returned with a bottle of Dutch gin. He poured two small glasses and they drank, emptying them at a swallow.

Kovalev was still staring in amazement.

'You should see your face,' said Van Louden.

Rarely in such an inhuman profession were there mo-

ments like this. Kovalev had not seen Van Louden—better
to continue thinking of him by that name—for nearly
ten years.

Van Louden was smiling at Kovalev's amazement.

'You like the look?'

Kovalev was not sure whether Van Louden meant the
look of himself or of the boat. He restricted himself to an
all-embracing 'yes' in reply.

The last time Kovalev had seen Van Louden they had
both been wearing shapeless suits and Van Louden had
been worrying about his hair thinning prematurely. Now
he wore a red silk shirt, tight at the waist, open wide at
the neck to display a silver medallion, and flared jeans.
His head was completely shaved and, like his face, it was
of the uniform brown that comes with the help of a sunlamp.

Van Louden spread his arms. 'It's the cool, hip
capitalist art dealer look!' He laughed, but Kovalev got
the feeling that he actually wanted to be admired.

Kovalev knew that Van Louden had gone abroad with
a false identity to set up an illegal network. Where, he had
not known.

'A *successful* capitalist art dealer by the look,' he said,
joining in the banter.

Van Louden snorted. 'Ah, it's easy to be a successful
capitalist provided you've got money to start with,' he
said. 'It's almost embarrassing. I open a gallery as cover
and it keeps making more and more money.'

Kovalev used a tone of mock seriousness. 'You must
adopt Marxist principles in running your gallery. Then
you can't fail to lose money. Otherwise you'll get corrup-
ted—and what's more we'll stop sending your pay.'

The two men enjoyed the glow of friendship for a few
more moments and then Kovalev forced himself to remember the urgency. 'I take it this place is safe?'

'As safe as I can make it. I search regularly.' He

shrugged. 'If it's not we're being watched anyway.'

'It's a wet affair,' said Kovalev.

Van Louden reacted without emotion.

'Who and when?'

'Just some fool. It needs to take place tomorrow.'

Although Van Louden said nothing, it was obvious what he was thinking: Kovalev had become too high-powered to be handling this kind of operation in person.

Kovalev sensed it but couldn't bring himself to admit the truth. 'I wasn't far away,' he said. 'Time was a problem. There seemed no one here ...'

'And it is important? That's why they risk you?'

'Perhaps.' With Van Louden, Kovalev thought he could relax. 'Either that, or someone has decided I'm now expendable.' He did not smile.

'How can I help?'

'What I want,' said Kovalev, 'what I need, is for one of your Palestinians to carry a case on an airplane for me. Can that be arranged?'

'Tomorrow morning?'

'Yes.'

Van Louden looked at his watch. 'I think so.' He stood. I'll drive you into town and make a phone call from a booth on the way.'

He paused before he reached the door.

'I take it there's a bomb in the parcel?'

'Yes,' replied Kovalev. 'But we don't have to tell him that, do we?'

At 10.35 p.m. Kovalev entered the hotel lobby. There was a message at the reception desk: 'Please call Mr Rutten.' A prearranged message from Sakulkin, only to be sent if there were problems.

Kovalev fought back his frustration. He had the number of a call booth he could call on the hour. There was nothing he could do for twenty-five minutes.

At eleven he telephoned from a booth in the lobby Sakulkin answered immediately. 'A message from home, he said.

'Tell me,' said Kovalev.

'Now? Over the phone?'

'We haven't time to play it by the book. Tell me fast and get off the line.'

The message tore apart all his planning. The Irish Special Branch had chosen just this moment to clamp down on Soviet diplomats suspected of helping the Irish Republican Army. It was being done according to diplomatic rules, of course: little things like delaying clearance of diplomatic pouches, or holding diplomats trying to leave the country while their credentials were 'checked' Kovalev's courier was one such man.

Kovalev walked back towards the elevator. Just over twelve hours. He would have to think again. Van Louden would be calling soon.

At the lobby shop he remembered he needed matches and he bought a throw-away lighter. While he waited for change he looked over the magazines. He found it astonishing how many of them dealt with war. He took his change and began to walk away.

A thought struck him and he turned back to the magazines. The cover of one, *A History of World War I in Forty Weekly Parts*, showed a shell exploding in a trench

Kovalev hurried for the elevator. It could still be done Inside his room he grasped his overnight case, opened it and examined the spot where the handles joined the body of the case. Satisfied, he placed it on the bed. The telephone rang.

'I need more help,' he told Van Louden. 'A laboratory . . .'

Van Louden picked him up an hour later. 'It's arranged, he said.

'Good.' Kovalev sank down in his seat.

'The firm specialises in customs-syntheses—making up chemical formulas on order for universities and research institutes, so its lab has virtually everything.'

Kovalev nodded his appreciation.

The factory was in darkness and lay back from the road. The man waiting at the door was nervous. He was small, and his face had a hangdog look, the features of someone permanently struggling to stay out of debt or retain his job or keep his wife. As they walked through the building his stage whisper had the edginess of near-hysteria.

'You will be out at six?' he said. 'You'll see everything looks the way it does now?'

He switched on the neon lights, and they entered the laboratory.

The other two stood just inside the door while Kovalev looked round. A tap was dripping into a basin and from outside he could just hear the rumble of heavy lorries on the road. There was a strong smell of sulphur.

He returned to the door. 'It will do very well,' he said.

Van Louden was questioning the small man. 'You've got everything I wanted?'

'Yes.' He gestured to a spot on one of the benches where chemicals and pieces of apparatus were already lined up.

'The picric acid?' asked Kovalev.

'Yes—but there's not much. The amount I was told you wanted. It's not used widely now.'

Kovalev knew that. Some doctors still used it for burns, but not many.

'Will it be missed?' asked Kovalev.

'No. There's always a lot of wastage. I can handle it.'

Satisfied, Kovalev walked over to the bench and checked his watch. It was nearly one o'clock.

'He's nervous,' Kovalev said when the little man had left.

'He'll be all right. It's the first time he's had to do anything like this. Normally we just want to know which universities and which research bodies are ordering what formulas . . .'

Kovalev had begun to check through the equipment. Satisfied, he reached for his overnight case. He took off his jacket and pulled his tie undone.

He realised Van Louden was asking whether he could stay. 'Stay? Oh yes. We'll keep each other awake.'

But it was obvious from Kovalev's face and manner that he would have no problem staying awake. At last he knew what he needed to do and he was doing it.

First he studied the materials on the bench: the jar of yellow crystals, the larger jar of what looked like sugar, the bottle of what could have been olive oil. There was also a small selection of tools and two tubes of adhesive, brought by Van Louden.

With the door closed there was no sound from outside. The only noises were the dripping of the tap and soft, indecipherable mutterings from Kovalev as he began to work.

Van Louden watched as Kovalev poured some of the oily liquid into a narrow jar. He then plugged the jar with a rubber cork and turned it upside down. He wanted to know how long the concentrated sulphuric acid would take to eat through the rubber.

Then he began to examine the case. It had two compartments, one for clothes and one for papers. The handle was hollow plastic, the ends protruded into the case. It was crudely finished.

Kovalev peeled back the lining material exposing the base of the handles. Then, using a piece of tubing, he filled the handles with water to see how much they would hold.

Half an hour had passed. The acid began to trickle through the rubber stopper on to the dish below. Kovalev noted the exact time and re-set the experiment, this time doubling the thickness of rubber.

So far he had said nothing. Now he began to speak, explaining his actions to Van Louden.

The bomb was going to be the case itself. The explosive would be packed along the top side of the case and the lining replaced over it. It would reduce the inside width of the case by about an inch, too small an amount for anyone to notice.

He began to mix the ingredients. First, the yellow crystals. It was the magazine that had made him think of them.

'This stuff has many names,' he explained, measuring a quantity of crystals. 'The British called it lyddite, the French melinite, the Italians pertite. Even the Japanese had their own name for it—shimosito.'

'Picric acid?'

'That's it.'

Kovalev was enjoying his lecture. He weighed a pound of the material. It looked like coloured granulated sugar.

'It was once very important,' he said. '*The* great explosive—more powerful than TNT. There was just one trouble, though. They filled bombs and shells and grenades with it—but it corroded the metal. Useless!'

To the picric acid he added a half pound of slightly dampish granules—'Sodium chlorate,' he said. He then added an equal amount of ordinary sugar.

He made the mixture into a block, the length of the case and about an inch wide, and put it into a makeshift container of cardboard and brown sticky paper.

He tried it for size on the inside of the case. A good fit.

'Now, we just stick it in there, re-seal the lining and ...'

'But how do you detonate it?'

'Ahhh ...'

The second lot of acid had burnt through its rubber cork.

'Concentrated sulphuric acid,' said Kovalev. 'We fill the handles with it, seal it with rubber, and wait for it to burn its way through the rubber. It won't burn through plastic.'

'And then . . .'

'And then,' repeated Kovalev.

He checked his watch. The acid had taken 77 minutes to work its way through.

He went silent.

'Problems?' asked Van Louden.

'I'd like thicker rubber,' said Kovalev. 'It burns through quicker than I'd like. But if I increase the amount of rubber there's not enough room for acid.'

He considered the problem. Finally he nodded. 'Yes, yes,' he assured Van Louden. 'There's a way . . .' It would have to be 77 minutes, but he would see the bomb was handed over at the last minute. The assassin would have to stay close to Zorin on the aircraft. Then if there were delays on the ground the blast itself would be enough to kill the man. He calculated that it would be fatal up to three rows of seats away.

Priming it immediately before the handover was no problem. He would put the bomb together now, the acid contained in a glass phial inside the handle. The ends of the handle would be plugged with rubber. To release the acid he would strike the handle hard enough to smash the glass. The only problem was the simple one of handing over the case to Van Louden's Palestinian.

He inserted the block of explosive and re-stuck the lining. He moved the case under a light. It looked untouched.

Van Louden was looking at his watch.

'You were quick,' he said. 'Our friend will be relieved.'

They began to walk towards the door. In anticipation of being outside and able to light a cigar, Kovalev took his new, throwaway lighter from his pocket.

He clicked it several times watching the flame flare and die. Each time there was the sound of a hiss of gas.

He stopped and stared at it, as though hypnotised. Van Louden watched amused. He tried to remember whether it was possible to buy such lighters in Russia, even in the special shops.

Kovalev turned back into the room and held the lighter underneath a lamp. After studying it for a few moments, he spoke. 'No. He said we'd got until six. I'd like to use the time.'

And clutching the lighter he turned back to the bench.

CHAPTER 18

They had decided that any news of developments should
go to Sunnenden. Scott wanted to know nothing—unless
things started to go wrong—until it was all over.

Cory—both Scott and Sunnenden agreed—was too
close to breaking down. Having set everything in motion
he seemed to have gone into a state of deep shock.

The last time Sunnenden had seen him he had been
slumped in his sitting room, his head leaning even further
to one side than usual, eyes blank and unseeing. His hands
were clasped tightly on his lap, and when he raised one to
beckon Sunnenden to sit it shook more than ever.

The other reason Scott had suggested news should be
relayed to Sunnenden, as the younger man well knew, was
to ensure that it was his head that remained on the block.
Scott would survive; there was always room for his special
talents. As for Sunnenden, there was already the suggestion that a posting with one of the US agencies abroad
might 'broaden' his experience.

Sunnenden reflected on this as he sat behind his desk
gazing around the room, wondering how much longer it
would remain his.

So far there had been only one message, a report of
Zorin's safe arrival in Holland from the CIA station
there. Sunnenden debated driving out to tell Cory, but
decided against it—seeing the man in his present state
only added to his depression.

Now at 11.30 a.m. he had nothing to do but wait
shuffle files that had only been sent to him 'for information', and wonder what to tell Janet. Could he persuade

her that an overseas posting was a promotion? He would have to tell her something—and soon. The previous evening they had fought right in front of the boys.

'Just *look* at you,' Janet screamed.

And he realised that his rumpled trousers—normally militarily creased—and unshone shoes were public announcements of his failure.

'Why? Why?' she had asked.

And Sunnenden had remained silent until she sent the boys away and then made up a bed for herself in the spare room.

He squared the files absentmindedly and straightened a pencil. He could not go out. He wanted to be at his desk when news arrived. He suddenly remembered that was one thing he could do.

The dissidents' file was still in his right, bottom drawer. He unlocked it. And then, painstakingly slowly, he fed the contents sheet by sheet through the shredding machine until only the empty folder remained.

When another message finally came it made no sense to Sunnenden. He used a scrambled telephone to call the CIA man who had been delegated to pass material to him.

'What's it mean? Is it important?'

The voice at the other end was curt; the tone made it clear he was co-operating only as far as he had to, that he found even that distasteful.

'Ask Cory,' said the man. And he hung up.

Cory felt he was coming through it. The more powerful anti-depressants that had been prescribed helped, but he thought it was more than that ...

At least he had done what he could. It wasn't his fault that the scheme would not go ahead. Of course, people were going to suffer—Zorin would probably die, his wife would be widowed, the child fatherless. But in the long term would things have really been any different for them? Cory was sure that, without hope of escape, Zorin would have returned to dissidence with vigour and reckless regard for himself—and would certainly have ended dying in a labour camp or enduring a living death.

And as for Parker, he would be better off than before. He would be got out of Moscow and Cory would ensure that he remained free.

Once Cory convinced himself all this was true, he even began to feel sorry for Sunnenden.

That was not easy. Throughout his life Cory, like all good intelligence men, had gloried in anonymity, of *not* seeking any public acclaim. For a man—no matter how ambitious—to risk an operation by behaving as Sunnenden had ...

But with his new calm Cory thought in time he might find some understanding for that too. What would he himself lose from all this? Really nothing. But Sunnenden? Cory had no doubt that even if the younger man survived he would no longer rise high inside government; too many people knew he had blown something even if they weren't sure what it was.

When Sunnenden did arrive, unexpected and unannounced in the mid afternoon, Cory was so anxious to appear sympathetic that it was some minutes before he heard the point of the visit.

Sunnenden handed him a slip of paper.

'I was told it would make sense to you.'

The message was short. A man called Kovalev, travelling under an assumed name on a German passport, believed to be on his way to a secret meeting of terrorists, had diverted at Brussels and entered Holland.

Out of habit Cory began to tear the paper into small pieces.

'Well, does it mean anything?'

'It means,' said Cory, wearily, 'that it's going according to plan.'

He wasn't through it. Perhaps he never would be.

The same message reached Scott.

Despite what he had told Sunnenden, Scott was not going to risk ignorance at what was going on this time. So, secretly, he arranged direct to get copies of all reports to Sunnenden.

In Scott's case, though, because they came from one of his highly placed 'young men' within the Company, they were accompanied by explanation.

The news was delivered to Scott by hand.

He nodded appreciatively. It *was* working.

His mind quickly reviewed what was happening and what was likely to happen.

He made a sudden decision. There was just one more thing to do. He picked up the telephone and began dialling.

CHAPTER 19

Zorin winced at the light and checked the time. It was only 6.30 a.m.

To relieve his tension he had drunk heavily the previous night. Now his hangover was coupled with anger at himself; he had been foolish to take the risk of drifting around bars near the hotel.

Now he was suffering for it. At seven he eased himself out of bed and, naked, walked across to the windows. There was a narrow balcony with an iron rail and he stood for a minute, looking down on the tram queues, before heading for the shower.

He turned it to cold. Afterwards he dressed slowly, studying himself in the mirror.

He still had not become accustomed to the face that looked back: the cropped hair, the moustache. Somehow, desperately, he wanted to revert to his natural self; he had a strange feeling that only once that happened would he be safe.

Tanya would be amused by the look though. He had tried not to anticipate their reunion. Even to think of it seemed to tempt fate. He forced himself to the thought that this, finally was *the* day.

Downstairs he sat in the glass-enclosed terrace, looking out at the Amsterdam Stock Exchange, drinking bitter black coffee.

He glanced through the *International Herald Tribune*. There had been a kidnapping in Ireland. Journalists were on strike in Rome. The Israelis and the Syrians were beginning their disengagement.

One story he read carefully. President Nixon, speaking to the graduating class of the Naval Academy in Annapolis, had come out strongly against those who advocated using détente to force Russia to take a new attitude to dissidents and to Jews who wanted to emigrate.

Zorin's lips moved with the text: 'We cannot gear our foreign policy to transformation of other societies.'

Zorin pushed the paper aside. The things that were done in the name of détente. Or was it because of Watergate? The one possibility that never struck him was that the President could have been making his speech—as a gesture to Russia—partly in the light of Zorin's own escape.

Normally on a Thursday morning at eight Daniel Raviv was still asleep. Lectures at the University of Amsterdam started late.

But the previous night he had received a call asking if he could help out in the Release Center for an hour or two. There he shared a table with Egmond, helping fold appeals into envelopes. For one moment they were alone.

'I think the time has come when you can help,' said Egmond, hardly able to contain the boyish excitement in his voice.

The meeting took place in the centre of Dam Square. Raviv was seated among the pigeons and the American hippies who had become a quaint part of Amsterdam culture but in reality could not leave because away from Holland they would lose their drug supplies.

Raviv was slight, bespectacled and had a mop of dark curly hair. He had a scar across his right temple, not quite hidden by his hair. Sometimes he fantasised that it had happened in a fight in which, finally, he had been victorious. In actuality he'd been tripped by another boy at school who thought Raviv cissy.

Raviv was a Jew and an Israeli. He was also a Marxist who hated the idea of Zionism and felt shame at the plight of the Palestinians. One day, after hearing Egmond arguing the Palestinian case with obvious passion, he had sought to catch Egmond alone and had then told him how much he agreed.

From that it had been one step to being asked if he would help if it ever proved necessary. It had also been impressed upon him that, in the meantime, the best way he could aid the cause was to hide his true feelings.

The man who approached him was, Raviv decided, probably Lebanese. Speaking as though Raviv's agreement to co-operate was a foregone conclusion, he explained that they needed Raviv to make a short return trip to Israel.

'There are some reports,' he explained, 'that *must* be delivered to our friends working under cover there. The papers look innocuous enough, but it is vital nothing is suspected. That is why we would prefer someone with an Israeli passport. What better reason for flying to Israel than one is going home?'

Raviv said nothing but his heart had begun to pound with excitement—a chance to help the cause, and an opportunity to gain a position of respect.

'Will you do it?' the man asked at last.

Raviv basked in the note of concern in the man's voice. They needed him!

He looked around the square, purposely delaying replying in order to gain the maximum pleasure from the moment. His look took in the Amsterdamers enjoying the sun, the tourists busily photographing him—the hippies. The puritan in him shuddered.

'Yes,' he said. 'Of course.'

At eight Kovalev was still asleep. Thirty minutes later he was wakened by the floor waiter with his breakfast. He ate hungrily, staring at the case. He pulled it towards him. A few hours before it looked all right, but what was it like in the light of day? He examined the lining, weighed it in his hand. He had done a good job.

Just before nine he received a telephone call. The shortage of time had limited the precautions that could be taken.

'I'm sorry to bother you so early,' said Van Louden, 'but I thought I should let you know that the artist agrees to your terms.'

'Good. I am most grateful. Perhaps I could collect the painting?'

'But of course,' replied Van Louden. 'Would the gallery at 9.30 be too early?'

It would have been more natural for Raviv to take the bus to the airport, but the man who had met him in Dam Square insisted he be driven. They wanted some time to brief him.

The mechanics were simple. He should wait until 10.30, follow the fat man into the post office and change cases with him. All he had to do then was take the flight and await further orders.

Van Louden, however, could not help extending the briefing. Raviv was an unknown quantity and without alarming him Van Louden wanted to ensure that he did not make any elementary mistakes. It would be disastrous if he were picked up at the airport.

The bomb would probably get through the guards. But both he and Kovalev knew that more potential hijackers or murderers were picked up because of their behaviour than because of what they carried.

A brief car journey did not allow much time, but it did provide a chance for the most basic guidance.

Van Louden did not do it himself. He decided against using Egmond or the Lebanese who had propositioned

Raviv in the square—both were known to hold radical views and he did not want the risk of the student being spotted arriving at the airport with either of them.

Instead he used a lecturer at the university, a Dutchman in his mid thirties, not known for his revolutionary beliefs. Raviv recognised him—but only as a teacher. His surprise was visible.

The lecturer explained to Raviv that he was not the only courier booked on the flight. He showed Raviv a Polaroid picture of Zorin, taken earlier that morning ostensibly by a tourist snapping the street as Zorin left his hotel. 'This is the man,' he said. 'You are to show no sign of recognising him, but you *must* stay close to him on the aircraft. It's a flight where they don't allocate seats in advance—passengers sit where they can—so you won't have that worry. Sometime before you arrive at Lod airport, he will pass you more instructions.'

The student listened intently, his excitement increasing with each now instruction. It was like being initiated into some secret society. By being briefed he was becoming someone special.

Then, as instructed, the man carefully checked Raviv's clothes and luggage: was it suitable for the flight destination? Was the luggage sufficient for the kind of trip that Raviv was ostensibly making? Many hijackers were caught because they paid no regard to these obvious points.

Then he gave Raviv a half dozen easily remembered pieces of advice. All of them had resulted from detailed research both in the USSR and in the United States— where the researchers were not only good but were also kind enough to publish their work in technical journals.

'I won't tell you to behave naturally,' said the man, 'because that's impossible. But we want you to avoid these few things.'

He listed them. Raviv was not to stand close to walls or pillars while waiting for his flight (a giveaway to security men that he wanted to hide). Nor should he move constantly round the shops and telephone booths. If anyone wanted to search his case he should not appear over-eager to help. Nor should he worry if they examined any of the papers inside. They would stand up to physical scrutiny; unless they were examined in a laboratory, where the microdots would be revealed, they would simply seem like university papers.

Nor, Raviv was told, should he ask a lot of questions about the flight—again an action that alerted security men.

The short briefing finished, the man began asking questions, checking Raviv's understanding of what he had said. Finally, as the car neared the airport, he nodded. He was satisfied.

The architect who designed Schipol airport decided it should be painted grey and white: the people, he said, should supply the colour.

Kovalev added his own colour to the scene that morning, Thursday, 6 June. He wore blue trousers, a pale blue shirt, and a bright check sports jacket, all brand new.

He carried the fibre-glass travel case somewhat gingerly. The chances of an accidental explosion were small, the mixture was stable. But explosives always made him nervous.

He had bought a ticket for Madrid and once past passport control and customs, he settled down in the departure lounge to watch the Post Office. It was little more than a counter selling stamps, run by one man who also worked a switchboard controlling calls from a line of telephone booths.

Kovalev had arranged the meeting with Raviv for as late as possible before the student had to make his way to the departure bay.

At 10.30 he walked to the Post Office desk and said he wanted to make a local call. He was directed to box number three and told to dial direct.

He leaned against the wooden partition separating him from the next booth. His call was to the hotel. While he waited for the switchboard to connect him with reception, he placed his case flat on the floor.

Reception answered. No, they told him, there were no messages.

As he thanked them, Kovalev saw Raviv arrive with a case identical to the one he carried, except for a red luggage tab.

The student passed and took the next booth.

Kovalev quickly glanced around to check no one could see—and brought his heel down hard on the handle of his case. He lifted it and shook it. Inside, he heard the fragments of glass rattle. The acid was now free to start eating through the rubber.

He waited for a few seconds and walked out, leaving his case on the floor.

'Is this your bag?' said the youngster, holding out a case.

'Oh yes, thank you. I'm always forgetting things.' Kovalev tore off the red tag as he walked towards the desk to pay for the call.

Zorin also arrived early. He had not wanted to but was afraid of missing the airplane.

His hangover had settled down to a faint heaviness. At the airport he welcomed the bustle and the anonymity of the crowds. He had to join a small queue to pass the border guards. One took his passport and handed it back without even looking up. Zorin was through into the departure lounge.

He killed some time by walking to the magazine and book stall. A photograph of a woman ballet dancer on the cover of one periodical reminded him of Tanya. He hurriedly bought a copy of *Time* and walked away.

The longing to be with Tanya was frightening in its intensity. He experienced that terrible feeling, triggered by flying, that he would never make it.

He felt a great desire to buy her something. The act of buying would be an act of faith—an expression of a certainty that he would be with her again soon. And something for the baby? Or was that tempting fate too much? While he had tried not to think of Tanya, he had tried doubly hard not to dwell on her pregnancy. He wanted freedom; he wanted her; and he wanted children.

He walked into the duty free shop and began wandering among the shelves.

Perfume, it had to be perfume.

He examined bottle after bottle; he tried to remember her tastes in Western perfumes. Someone had once given her *Femme* and he remembered she had liked that. But when she went abroad herself she had bought something different. He could not quite remember. Was it Guerlain? He thought perhaps it was. The bottle had the same elaborate shape.

The choosing became a complex problem. He let it take over from his fear and other emotions. Picking the right perfume became the most important thing.

Someone was pushing him, trying to get past. He started.

Back to reality. He decided on Dior. He bought it together with Dutch gin in an ornate bottle and two boxes of Carl Upmann Blues. He paid and watched the girl at the cash desk stamp his green boarding card.

Carrying his bag he walked back into the lounge. There was still time to kill. He walked around the lounge.

On impulse, he bought a tiny teddy bear, no more than perhaps three inches high, from a stand of toys at the newspaper stall. Almost embarrassed, he pushed it into his pocket. The dull feeling had given way to one of tense nervousness. He sidled close to the pillars. Surely the man in the blue suit had been watching him for the past few minutes. Zorin tried to glance without making it apparent. Yes, the man was looking; now he was coming towards him. Zorin felt his hands tighten, felt the sickness in his stomach. A woman and small child crossed in front of Zorin. The man grasped the child's hand, and the three began to walk towards a departure gate.

10.35—almost time for the call. He watched the monitor screens. He realised he was smoking without remembering he had lit a cigarette. A drink? He knew he was being stupid. A drink would help. He went over to the bar and ordered a large brandy and then stood almost reluctant to drink it once the glass was in his hand.

First the message was in Dutch, then Hebrew, finally in English. 'Flight KL525 is now boarding at gate C38 ...' He waited five minutes until he heard an announcement of the final call, then downed his brandy and walked towards C pier.

Unlike the pier he had used on his arrival, C pier had no moving walkway. There were seats in the middle and on the sides, and low partitions that divided off departure areas for individual flights.

C38 was right at the end. Zorin passed building work going on for a fourth pier.

He showed his boarding pass and was allowed through into the sealed off section. The flight was almost full: 207 passengers stood and sat waiting to be checked.

The check was taking a long time. There was a group of Chassidic Jews with their full beards and ear curls who came in for special scrutiny—what better disguise? One began to argue. A plainclothes guard came forward and asked a quick series of questions in Hebrew. The answers seemed to satisfy him and he nodded to guards to clear them.

Zorin felt near-hysteria envelop him. Travelling by underground railway or crossing a bridge over a river there was sometimes a magnetic draw to jump. He felt a similar emotion now. He found himself wanting to step forward and confess, 'My name is not Leonard Rose. I am not an American. I am Alexandrai Leonidovich Zorin. You think I am in Moscow, but I am here . . .'

He joined the queue. The guards were thorough. Each passenger had to open his baggage. Then it was X-rayed. There was a body search, for most a quick frisk but for a few a more thorough check behind a screen.

The guard opened Zorin's box of duty-free gin, asked him his nationality, stared at his face for a few long moments. Then he was through, on to the enclosed ramp and the stretched DC8.

He chose a seat near the centre of the airplane, on the aisle. As he sat, he was conscious of some jostling for the seat behind him. He took the magazine from the rack on the back of the seat in front of him. He skimmed through an article on Van Gogh. Other passengers were still boarding.

Behind him, a young man had seated himself. Zorin felt the man pushing a small case forward beneath his seat. The aircraft seemed to be taking an endless time to fill.

It was 11.25. By now the aircraft, which was due to leave at 11.30, should have been beginning to taxi out on the runway. It was still attached to the pier, and the last passengers were boarding.

Raviv was trying to read a newspaper but could not concentrate. He wondered what was in the case and how much his actions would advance the cause and whether this was just the start. He looked at the back of Zorin's seat. When would the man make contact?

Zorin had closed his eyes. The brandy had mellowed him. He was thinking of Tanya. He realised someone was talking to him. It was a stewardess. First she tried Dutch, then English. It took a little time to focus. '. . . and if you wouldn't mind, it would be nice . . .' At last he realised he was being asked if he would change his seat; something to do with two people who wanted to sit together.

He followed the stewardess along the aisle. He was a dozen rows away, beginning to edge himself into his seat, the aircraft still grounded, when the bomb went off.

The sound came first, drowning every other noise, awful in its suddenness.

Before there was time to react, the blast-wave hit. It struck Zorin hard, pitching him forward into the aisle. As he fell, the right side of his face hit the edge of a fold-down table that had been forced away from the seat ahead. But he felt nothing. It was like a dream being acted in slow motion.

After the blast there was a silence, and Zorin found himself thinking that if this was death there was nothing to fear.

Then, almost simultaneously, came the cracks of pieces of broken aircraft and luggage hitting the sides of the cabin—and the screams.

Zorin felt people beginning to move around him. Terrified that he would be trampled to death, he managed to get to his knees, screaming and shouting now but not realising it.

He turned towards the site of the blast. The cabin lights had gone out; the immediate scene was lit by daylight that entered through a jagged hole in the ceiling. The air was full of small pieces of fluttering paper and material. Some of them were alight.

He gazed at it all, seeing but not feeling.

Then his mind opened itself to the screams and the people and the smell of burning. He could just make out what must be bodies—a beam of light picked out a hand, incredibly white, lying limp over the edge of a seat.

As Zorin watched, a body rolled over into the aisle. He could see only its shape, but there was something strange about the head. Zorin could not know: it was Raviv, a seven-inch-long piece of metal embedded in his skull.

He saw a stewardess emerge from the smoke. The heat produced by the released gases, over two thousand degrees Fahrenheit, had set fire to her uniform. She stumbled down the aisle, her hands to her face, flames leaping from her hair and clothes.

Her mouth was open, gasping. But Zorin could hear nothing from her—other screams, continuous, high-pitched, drowned them.

He began to clamber for the door. Another stewardess was vainly trying to hold people back.

For the first time Zorin felt the blood pouring down the side of his face. Yet even as he struggled and pushed, realisation welled up inside him.

The explosion must have taken place within feet of where he had been sitting. He had been the target. Someone had tried to kill him. Suddenly he was out of the aircraft, back on to the bridge linking it with the pier. His feet echoed on the corrugated iron.

On the pier he finally sank to the ground and began to sob. A group gathered round him. Police were flooding into the area. Someone was saying 'Get him somewhere quiet' and another 'No, don't move him.' But two men lifted him and carried him behind one of the partition walls.

There he lay, a coat under his head, hidden from the crowds who were now just sounds. Now the men who had carried him were being ushered away. Someone was wiping the blood from his face and talking in Dutch.

'Help me, help me,' Zorin whispered.

Despite the panic his mind was working. He knew what

he would do now. They had tried to murder him, but he had survived.

He had been crazy to follow instructions. What did he owe anyone? Why should he do what he was told? All that mattered was staying alive, and Tanya.

He would learn from his mistake. He would go to the Dutch authorities or the American embassy and surrender himself. They would protect him and get him to Israel. He would take no more risks.

'You're all right. Fine. Hardly hurt,' said a voice in English. The words were meant to be reassuring, not factual: the facial cut was superficial but Zorin looked as though he had been trampled on; there might be internal injuries or broken ribs.

'I'm a doctor,' he explained. 'Airport emergency.'

The doctor pulled a bag towards him and took out a hypodermic. This case would keep. There were obviously more serious ones at the site itself.

Zorin stared at the hypodermic. He tried to lift his arms. 'No! No!' His voice was full of horror.

The doctor was impatient to move on. 'Only to help you ... Come on.'

A second face joined the doctor's in Zorin's vision. For the first time he realised there was another man present, a border policeman in his blue shirt and trousers.

Zorin could not understand what was being said, but finally the doctor put away the hypodermic and stood. He paused for a moment, reluctant, and then smiled. 'You'll be fine,' he said to Zorin in English. 'Just fine. I'll be back soon.' Then he was gone.

The policeman took his place. He was a big man. Kneeling was obviously difficult. 'I told him go tend the rest and I'd stay with you.'

Zorin smiled his thanks. He felt safe. The guard pulled aside his gun holster and fumbled.

'Cigarette?' He held out the packet.

Zorin tried to extract one and failed. The policeman placed one in his mouth. Zorin saw him look up and around. Then the policeman offered his lighter. Zorin watched it come close. It was bright yellow, just a cheap throw-away lighter. He suddenly realised it had passed the end of the cigarette and was under his nose. The policeman spoke. Zorin looked up, surprised. He had spoken in Russian. The man had his face half-turned away and it looked as though he was holding his breath. Then Zorin felt the jet of cold spray and gasped as the bitter sweetness filled his nostrils. His body tried to arch, but a hand was being pushed hard against his chest.

He was dead within thirty seconds.

Still holding his breath Kovalev rose and walked out on to the main pier. He looked back. The body, pushed close against the far side of the partition, could not be seen. In the chaos he thought there should be at least fifteen minutes, but five would do. In the air-conditioning the vapour, which was very slightly lighter than air anyway, would have completely dispersed by then. Not even that odour variously described as peach-blossom or bitter almond would remain around the body. And in practice very few people could detect the smell anyway.

Kovalev took a deep breath. He did not think he had inhaled any of the vapour. He had certainly not taken in enough to kill, but he would be nervous for the next hour or so, watching for warning signs of a small dose—the watering eyes, the headache, the salivating mouth, the irritated throat.

Perhaps better to be absolutely safe. As he walked he took an ampoule from his pocket and broke it into a handkerchief. He lifted the cloth and inhaled deeply. He gasped at the amyl nitrite and felt his heart begin to pound.

Kovalev neared the departure lounge. Men working on

the new fourth pier had gathered together and were talking excitedly and staring towards the scene of the explosion.

He turned and walked through them. Beyond was the room where the men changed from outside clothes into overalls. Hooks were covered with jackets. Against one wall were lockers where the workmen left their belongings.

Kovalev took a brightly checked jacket from the hook where he had left it earlier and slipped it on.

The third locker from the top on the extreme left was unlocked, as arranged. From it he took his travel case, leaving the black holster in its place. That would be collected later.

No one looked as he walked out.

The man who entered the departure lounge seconds later was no longer a policeman, but a tourist.

There was not much to do now. He'd have to get rid of the empty lighter. Any drain would do for that. It was, after all, a throw-away lighter.

As such, it had intrigued him from the start. It was an almost perfect poison spray. He had converted it partly as a second line of attack, and partly because he found himself with the time and the right equipment and chemicals.

He was glad he had. A lot had obviously gone wrong. The aircraft had been delayed. And the bomb had gone off ten minutes earlier than he had planned. And the case could not have been near Zorin.

But throughout his career he had always tried to anticipate failures—and to have a standby scheme ready to put into action.

It had been such a simple idea. He had drilled a hole in the bottom of the liquid gas container and drained out the liquid. He replaced this with hydrocyanic gas in liquid form, mixed with a fluorocarbon propellant he had found in the laboratory.

The other modifications were minimal. He removed the flint and slightly enlarged the valve so that more gas would emerge when the lighter was worked.

Suddenly his legs felt tired. He found an empty bench and sat. The elation started to diminish. He realised how close he had been to failing—and no matter how important you were failure never went unpunished.

But he hadn't failed! He began to feel contentment again, and then suddenly and unexpectedly, he pictured a body—a man lying hurt, eyes questioning. Kovalev shuddered. It *had* been a long time since he had been operational. For a few seconds he felt pity and disgust, and then he forced them down. He had done what he had to.

CHAPTER 20

'Hey,' she said, and leaned forward to kiss his forehead.

Parker turned on to his side, rolling himself in the blanket, revelling in the dream.

She kissed his forehead again.

Parker opened his eyes. Anna was leaning over him, smiling. She was wearing a white nylon nightdress, the front decorated with frills. By Western standards it was very short— a good three inches above the knee. She had produced it from the bottom of a chest the previous evening. 'My decadent reminder of the West,' she had told him, lifting it high in front of her as she crouched on her knees.

Parker had not asked 'reminder of what?'

He sat up and took the cup of black coffee that she held out to him. He sipped it immediately, with pleasure; he had been in Russia long enough to know what a rare delight fresh coffee was.

'Come back to bed,' he urged.

Anna looked at her watch. Then, almost coyly, she slid back under the covers. They both, Parker realised, smelled of sweat and sex.

'Where's your coffee?' he asked.

'I drank it.'

Parker was not sure whether she was telling the truth or whether there had only been enough for one. Whichever way, he by-passed the answer.

'Let me put my head on your shoulder,' he said.

Anna leaned back against the pillow, and Parker eased himself until his head rested on her breast, her arm round him.

'Nice?'

'Mmm.'

'I'll miss you,' she said at last.

'Me too.'

They lay still for perhaps five minutes and then Anna shrugged and pulled herself up. 'I must get ready.'

Parker made no move to stop her. Sitting up nursing his cup, now half empty, he watched her begin to dress.

'Must you really go tomorrow?'

'You know so.'

She was naked now, but with her back towards him, shy at showing her breasts. They had made love each time in the dark.

When she finished dressing, she turned to face him. She wore a patterned dress, red with white flowers. It was too young for her, but he smiled his approval.

'You'll get yourself breakfast?' He nodded.

She left a few minutes later. He was still in bed. 'Till tonight.' She blew a kiss from the door.

Parker rose minutes later. The apartment was almost unnaturally quiet. He found eggs and boiled two. It felt strange being alone. He could still smell sex on himself. He washed in the kitchen sink while the eggs boiled, not daring to use the communal bathroom on the landing below.

After eating he checked his watch. It was 8.50. Parker reached deep into his breast pocket and took out the photograph of Susan that Cory had given him in London. He stared at her for a long time. Her eyes were almost impossibly blue.

It took him a little while to find paper. Using the back of a brown paper bag, he wrote hesitantly in Russian: 'Thanks,' in large letters. And then he added, 'I'll never forget you.' He propped it on the kitchen table.

It was a task of only minutes to pack his Air Canada bag. He took great care in tying on the bright red address label—a precautionary touch added by Cory. The idea was that if the militia were harassing visitors arriving at the embassy, as they sometimes did, the Marine guards on duty could easily pick out Parker and escort him inside.

Even though both elevators were now working, he took the stairs to the street. The morning rush was over and there were few people at the Metro station.

It was 9.45 when he emerged into the street again. There was a fine drizzle and he enjoyed the feel of it on his face.

He was to arrive at the gate to the embassy at 9.55. His timing, he realised, was perfect.

At 9.50 the American embassy compound came into sight. Parker stood on the far side of the road, facing the heavy iron gates behind which stood the old, nine-storey building.

Near by he could see the militiamen who stood on duty twenty-four hours a day to 'protect the embassy from vandals and gatecrashers.' They were chatting together, taking no special notice.

Parker waited for a lull in the traffic and began to cross the street. On his right he saw the doors of a parked car open. It was grey. Four men got out. From their manner and their clothes, Parker knew immediately that they were KGB men. They began to walk in his direction.

He felt a stab of fear but did not change his pace: he was on the sidewalk near the embassy and the KGB men were still fifty yards away.

Parker neared the gate to the compound, conscious now that his heart was pounding, not with effort but with nervousness. He looked back over his right shoulder. The men were still walking in his direction, spread out four abreast, not hurrying at all.

The gate was no more than ten yards away now. Behind it, he could see a US Marine guard. There was no reason, but Parker quickened his pace.

In seconds he would be safe. He felt his mouth forming into a smile. He wanted to giggle hysterically.

He watched the guard focus in his Air Canada bag with its tag. He thought he saw recognition in the man's eyes.

Parker looked back again. The KGB men were still keeping up their slow steady pace. Then he realised that the Marine guard had moved.

The guard slammed the lock on the gate, turned, and marched away.

Parker could not know, but from 8,000 miles away Scott had made sure there were no loose ends.

At first Parker could not believe it. He reached the gate and grabbed the bars with both hands. He pushed, but nothing would give. He pushed again. He looked back. The four men were nearer. Parker sank to his knees, his arms spread above his head, his hands tight round the bars. He began to bang his head against the gate.

Then he heard the footsteps.

PETER ISRAEL

THE STIFF UPPER LIP

It says Public Relations on the card, but make no mistake — B.F. Cage is a private eye, California style.

Hard-hitting investigator B.F. Cage was no ordinary bodyguard. But at six feet seven inches tall, and every inch packed with muscle, Roscoe Hadley was no ordinary body. France's number one basketball star, Hadley was a man with a following. And the following just happened to include the Mafia.

League-fixing, drugs-running — these days the Mob were into sporting ventures in a big way. Cage had to keep ahead of the game. And whatever the game was, it sure the hell wasn't cricket . . .

CORONET BOOKS

ERIC CLARK

THE SLEEPER

'Lie low, wait, do nothing until you hear from us. First you must establish yourself . . .'

Since these words, nearly thirty years ago, James Fenn – hero of the 1956 Hungarian uprising, one-time top Fleet Street journalist and KGB 'sleeper' agent – has been waiting to be called. From his Mediterranean island home he has almost forgotten his Soviet masters.

A world away in London, British security services are forced to investigate one of the Prime Minister's closest advisers – an industrialist suspected by the CIA of passing secrets to the Russians.

Fenn's time finally comes, and they must wake the sleeper . . .

'Straight into the top flight of spy-story writers'
Coventry Evening Telegraph

'Clark hits just the right pitch in his descriptions of a man caught in the prongs of having to follow orders or be exposed'
Book Buyer

CORONET BOOKS

MORE ADVENTURE & SUSPENSE
FROM CORONET

All these books are available at your local bookshop or newsagent, or can be ordered direct from the publisher. Just tick the titles you want and fill in the form below.

Prices and availability subject to change without notice.

CORONET BOOKS, P.O. Box 11, Falmouth, Cornwall.
Please send cheque or postal order, and allow the following for postage and packing:

U.K.—One book 30p, 15p for the second book plus 12p for each additional book ordered, up to a maximum of £1.29.

B.F.P.O. and EIRE—30p for the first book, 15p for the second book plus 12p per copy for the next 7 books; thereafter 6p per book.

OTHER OVERSEAS CUSTOMERS—50p for the first book plus 15p per copy for each additional book.

Name ....

Address ....

....